The Case of The Shrinking Shopkeeper
& Other Stories

T.G. Campbell

All characters in this collection of short stories are fictional. Any resemblance to persons living or dead is purely coincidental.

ALSO BY THE AUTHOR

The Case of The Curious Client
The Case of The Lonesome Lushington
The Case of The Spectral Shot
The Case of The Toxic Tonic

The Case of The Peculiar Portrait & Other Stories
The Case of The Russian Rose & Other Stories
The Case of The Gentleman's Gambit & Other Stories

TABLE OF CONTENTS

The Case of the Shrinking Shopkeeper

I

"I'm at my wit's end, Miss Trent."

"It *is* an unusual predicament you've found yourself in, Mr Foggity. When did you first notice something was amiss?"

"At the beginning of last week," he frowned. "No, one moment," he counted on his fingers. "Yes, it was the Tuesday before last." Mr Emmanuel Foggity was in his mid-fifties, but his youthful complexion and brilliant, chestnut-brown hair veiled this fact. Neat brows and strong cheekbones framed his lively, light-blue eyes. Pale lips, topped by a wax-coated moustache, were nibbled upon as he watched Miss Rebecca Trent write her notes.

The Bow Street Society clerk wore a light-weight jacket over a high-necked, plain-white shirt. A tie, secured into a large Eaton knot, rested between the broad lapels of the former. Both tie and jacket were forest-green to compliment the season. Though already slim, Miss Trent's figure was nevertheless exaggerated by the synching of her clothes and the contours of her tight, corset undergarment. Her own brown hair had been tied into a neat French braid and hung between the excess fabrics of her jacket's mutton-chop sleeves. Mr Foggity's attire, on the other hand, was far less elaborate—a light-grey suit with matching waistcoat and tie over a pristine, white shirt. The collar of the last was broad and so heavily starched, his Adam's apple caught upon it each time he swallowed.

The sounds of birdsong and passing carriages drifted upon a light breeze through the half-raised sash window of the Society's parlour. Miss Trent's notebook, knees, and feet were bathed in golden sunlight as she wrote. Though a handful of furniture had recently been added—a sofa by the hearth, a dresser, and armchairs in which the two sat—the room remained cavernous.

"I've never been a tall man," Mr Foggity went

on, "but to shrink as quickly as I have isn't natural, is it?" He simultaneously lifted his hands and shoulders for a moment. "Yet, my doctor has sworn to me on his reputation as a man of medicine that I'm *not* shrinking." Holding his knees, he leant forward. "Am I mad, Miss Trent?"

"I certainly believe you're convinced something is happening to you, Mr Foggity." She rested her hand upon the notebook and met his gaze. "Whether it's madness or not is something that remains to be seen by our members."

"Does this mean you'll accept my case?"

"It does." She rose. "If you would wait here, I'll telephone some members and ask that they come here to speak with you as soon as possible."

"*Thank you,* Miss Trent. Of course!" The clouds shifted and his face was at once lit up by sunlight.

II

Almost three quarters of an hour had passed when Miss Trent returned to the parlour. Behind her came a lady whose immense height gave Mr Foggity cause to frown. Her naturally dark-blond, wavy, hair was pinned up on her head's crown to create a sculpted style that continued to the nape of her neck. She wore a navy-blue, loose-fitting blouse adorned with a white, blossom pattern. Over the top of this, she wore a thigh-length, baby-blue coat similar in style to Miss Trent's. Her skirts, made of plain black cloth, hung down from her hips and ended at her ankles. Entering the room behind her was a gentleman with golden-blond curls, green eyes, and handsome features. The cut of his black frock coat and matching suit suggested they were tailor made and therefore, expensive. Finally, a burgundy-coloured waistcoat and cravat and a gold tie pin added colour to his appearance. Miss Trent moved to the side and, facing the newcomers, introduced, "Mr Percy Locke and his wife, Doctor Lynette Locke, Mr Foggity. They shall investigate your case."

"Doctor?" their client enquired while shaking Mr Locke's hand.

Without pause, and with great conviction, Dr Locke challenged, "Does my being a woman concern you?"

"No, no, no," Mr Foggity stumbled, shaking his head. Dr Locke, suspecting she hadn't yet convinced him, said, "I can assure you I have all the necessary credentials."

"I have no doubt of it," Mr Foggity answered. Dr Locke's mouth twitched into a smile.

"Good, because I'd like to examine you to eliminate physical illness as the cause for your sudden shrinkage." As she turned upon her heel and marched from the room, she added, "This way, please, Mr Foggity."

"Y—yes, of course." He cast a wary, backward glance at Miss Trent and followed. Miss Trent gave a nod of reassurance but released a small sigh as soon as he'd left.

"What is your opinion of him?" she enquired, turning toward Mr Locke.

"He is frightened," Mr Locke replied and took a turn around the room. After a moment, he remarked, "I see you have made great strides with the décor."

"Funds are limited—as you well know," Miss Trent countered, her arms folding across her chest. "Do you think he's being honest about his plight?"

"It is too early to say." He ran a leather-clad finger along the shelf above the hearth. Miss Trent had noticed Mr Locke had refrained from removing his gloves when he'd first arrived. Since he was such a stalwart in his adherence to the etiquette of polite society, Miss Trent had thought this odd. Yet, she'd decided against confronting him due to the circumstances. While she sat upon the sofa, he enquired, "The new lock I had installed is sufficient, I trust?"

"I had to let you in, didn't I?" she enquired, summoning a smirk to Mr Locke's features.

"My dear Miss Trent, even *I* would not attempt to pick a lock in broad daylight with a busy thoroughfare at my back and a police station up the street."

"I'd have thought the risk would be too irresistible to you, Mister Locke," Miss Trent half-taunted. Mr Locke's eyes seemed to twinkle in response as he settled beside her.

"While it *is* true I thrive on danger, I am not a fool—as you know."

"There is no sign of any physical illness which may cause Mr Foggity's sudden decline in height," Dr Locke announced as she breezed back into the room. Mr Foggity, who was putting his jacket on, reappeared a moment after. Dr Locke went on, "We must therefore look elsewhere for answers." She faced their client, "Mr Foggity, can you give us some examples of incidences which have led you to believe you're shrinking?"

"Yes… of course," he paused to accept Mr Locke's invitation to sit. Mr Locke, whom had risen upon his wife's return, took the other armchair while Dr Locke claimed his place beside Miss Trent. "I'm a confectioner by trade," Mr Foggity continued when they were all seated. "I have my own little shop on Oxford Street which I run with the help of my wife and a young assistant, Mr Huddleston. Behind my counter, there are some shelves with jars on them." Mr Foggity lifted his hand above his head as if reaching for something. "The Tuesday before last, I tried to take down a jar of Lemon Peel for a customer. They were on the top shelf but I could barely reach it." His hand dropped to his knee. "I'd never had problems reaching it before. Fortunately, I was able to wrap my hands about it by getting onto the ends of my toes - but that method was put paid to soon enough."

"Oh?" Mr Locke probed.

"Well, just *two* days later, I was asked to take down the same jar, again for a customer. Only, I had to use a *stool* to reach it. I must've looked quite the sight." He leant forward a little. "I just couldn't believe it. You see, when I realised my fingertips couldn't even *brush* the glass, I didn't know what to do with myself. My customer was the impatient kind. I balanced on the stool, took down the jar, and spilt half the peel onto the counter while I was weighing it."

"Aside from being unable to reach the jar, has anything else occurred?" Mr Locke enquired.

The shopkeeper replied, "It *has*. Mr Locke, if you could see my wife and me together then you would know she's but a half inch taller than I—usually. Since the Tuesday before last though, she's been towering over me more and more. She tells me she's grown no more since her younger years. Then there was the time at breakfast."

"Go on," Mr Locke urged, instinctively leaning toward their client in return.

Mr Foggity wrung his hands a moment and, looking between them all, stated, "You will all think it quite ridiculous. Perhaps I am going mad after all."

"Mr Foggity, something is quite clearly occurring which is causing you to think this way," Mr Locke reassured. "We cannot reach the truth of things, however, if you blindside us to certain goings on."

Their client frowned but, after receiving a gentle nod from Miss Trent, went on, "My Wife and I had spent a couple days away from London—at the seaside, in fact. I'd hoped the air would help clear my mind. When we came home, all was well and I thought that, perhaps, I had been imagining it all. The very next morning, however, I sat down to breakfast and my fears were realised all over again. Where my knees had touched the underside of the table previously, they were suddenly a good inch beneath. I gave Amy quite the start when I leapt up in terror."

"We must visit your shop and home at once," Mr Locke announced as he stood. "I trust they are both housed in the same location?" he enquired, striding toward the door. The others simultaneously hurried to join him.

Mr Foggity, perplexed, replied, "Y—Yes, but… Do you know what's happening to me, Mister Locke?"

"I believe I may." Mr Locke put on his top hat and enquired from his wife, "Don't we, darling?"

"I'm beginning to see it, yes," Dr Locke replied with a smile. Turning to the confused Mr Foggity, she added, "We shall have this matter resolved before the day is out."

"My carriage is waiting outside." Mr Locke opened the front door. "Shall we?"

III

It took some time for the Locke's carriage to traverse the traffic passing up and down Oxford Street. The familiar façade of a certain department store caused the two Bow Streeters to exchange glances while Mr Foggity, sitting across from them, remained oblivious to its existence. Instead, he stared out the opposite window and tapped his knees with each finger in turn. Yet, when the carriage finally stopped outside the unassuming little sweet shop, he sprung from his seat and leapt out with great haste.

"It shouldn't be closed," he said as he crossed the pavement and peered at a small sign hanging on the door's interior. He turned back to the carriage and, while Mr Locke assisted his wife in alighting, added, "Mr Huddleston was to look after the shop while I was away." Fumbling around in his pockets, Mr Foggity soon laid claim to his key—only to drop it with a clang. Bending over, without thought for propriety in the presence of a lady, the sweet shop owner snatched up his key from the step and opened the door.

The shop beyond was in darkness. A rosewood-panelled counter, approximately four feet high, stood to the rear of the small space. Behind it was a second counter of equal height lined with glass jars sealed with thickset lids. These lids had small, glass balls on their tops for one to grip while pulling open the containers. Above these jars was a set of three shelves housed within a wall-mounted, wooden box. Like the counter beneath them, each shelf had lines of glass jars occupying them. Handwritten labels, affixed to the glass, gave the name of the confectionary stored within. Among the delicacies on offer were Superior Conversation Lozenges, Fairy Rock, Violet Lozenges, Twisted Barley Sugar, and, of course, the offending Lemon Peel. As previously described by Mr Foggity, the peel was to be found on the top shelf. The main counter had more jars standing to attention along its front edge, again containing all manner of sweet goods, along with an impressive, brass register, a set of scales, and a pile of paper bags. Another counter stood against the walls to one's left and right with more shelves above them. These shelves were mounted directly into the wall, however. Each one of these additional shelves and counters were brimming with jars, boxes of jellies, and even lemonade.

"Amy?!" Mr Foggity called. Walking behind the main counter, he opened a door and peered inside. "I don't understand it," he said, closing it again. "There's no one here."

Mr Locke, whom had entered the shop behind its keeper, turned to his wife, "Would you be so kind as to search the back rooms, darling?"

"Certainly, darling." Dr Locke placed her Gladstone bag upon the counter beside the register and carefully stepped around Mr Foggity to enter the back rooms.

"Pardon me, but is that *absolutely* necessary?" Mr Foggity called after her.

"It is, I am afraid," Mr Locke answered directly behind him.

The shopkeeper at once spun around, "Mr Locke, I didn't hear you coming—"

"My wife and I have a strong suspicion about what is occurring here but, before we may explain further, we must have evidence to support our theory." Retrieving the stool from beneath the counter, Mr Locke placed it beside the back counter. Satisfied with its position, he next removed his frock coat, carefully folded it, and laid it across the front.

As he climbed up onto the stool, Mr Foggity enquired, "What are you looking for?"

"Evidence." Mr Locke slid a jar from the middle shelf positioned beneath his chest, and passed it down to his client. After bending over and spending several moments inspecting the underside of the top shelf in silence, he went on, "Tell me of Mr Huddleston; his relationship to you, his background, if there were any disagreements between you."

"We've not disagreed on anything to my knowledge. Godfrey's a good boy. He came to us after his father died. He'd taught Godfrey all he knew about carpentry—that was his trade, you see—but when he passed on, Godfrey had to sell all his father's tools to make ends meet. Well, the money he got from those didn't last long, so he decided to find himself a new trade. I was looking for an apprentice at the time and he proved to be a hard worker." Mr Foggity scratched his head when Mr Locke ducked down to peer at the underside of the very bottom shelf. "Godfrey's worked for me for over a year now. He's become like a son to me and Amy. It never happened for us—children. We've never known why and, course, with Amy's advancing years, it's unlikely to now."

"I found this in the pocket of an apron in the kitchen," Dr Locke informed the two as she returned, holding a scrap of paper. Giving it to her husband, she explained, "It's an advertisement for a cobbler. Mr Foggity, has your wife had her shoes mended recently?"

"No," their client replied. "She means to take mine though. Is it important?"

"That would depend on the condition of your wife's shoes," Dr Locke replied. "May I see them?"

"When she gets back, you may. She only owns the one pair."

"I see," Dr Locke paused. "Have your clothes become larger since you noticed your decrease in height?"

"Not that I've noticed," Mr Foggity replied as he lifted his arms and shifted his weight from side to side while looking down at himself. Dr Locke at once took hold of his jacket's lapel and, opening the garment, checked its interior. A soft hum left her lips but no further explanation was offered as she released it and took back the newspaper clipping from her husband.

Mr Locke, who had retrieved his frock coat after reading the advertisement, now put it on while walking into the kitchen. Discovering a square table, surrounded by three chairs, he enquired, "Is this where you eat breakfast?"

"It is, but I—what *are* you doing, Mr Locke?" the sweet shop owner enquired, stunned, as Mr Locke dropped onto his hands and knees, and crawled underneath the table. Feeling a gentle hand upon his arm, Mr Foggity looked to Dr Locke who said, "Do not worry. I promise you that all will be well soon enough."

"Darling, will you look at this, please?" Mr Locke requested, returning to his feet. With a small nod, Dr Locke crossed to him and then leant forward to peer under the table when he pointed something out.

"Ah, yes," she straightened. "It all makes perfect sense now—at least as far as the how is concerned. But why would someone go to such lengths?"

"What is it?" Mr Foggity enquired, moving forward but having his view of the table blocked by the two Bow Streeters. "What have you found?"

"Evidence which proves you are neither shrinking nor suffering an illness of the mind," Dr Locke replied. "Unfortunately, the 'why' still eludes us, however," Mr Locke added with a slight frown.

"The why doesn't matter, Mr Locke," their client said, smiling. "I'm *not* shrinking! *Thank* you! My wife will be ever so pleased!"

No sooner had these words left his lips, however, did the jangling of the shop's bell reach their ears. It was at once followed by a woman's yell, compelling the three to vacate the kitchen and investigate. As he went, Mr Foggity cried, "That's my wife! Amy!"

"*Stop* him! Keep him away from me!" Mrs Foggity, a middle-aged, buxom brunette with a jet-black mark around her left eye, wailed from behind a constable when they emerged. The pair was accompanied by a man in his early-twenties with strawberry-blond, wiry hair thinning on top and a pale, freckle-covered complexion. All three were in turn standing in a triangle formation in the middle of the shop. Mrs Foggity continued, "He's gone *mad! Arrest him!* He's the *scoundrel* who struck me!"

"Amy…" Mr Foggity began, but his voice faded and he stared at his wife in disbelief. "I have *never* struck you. In all our years of marriage I have only—"

"He's lying! I told him he wasn't shrinking and he struck me!"

"Godfrey, you know I would never harm my Amy," Mr Foggity pitifully pleaded with his assistant.

Yet the subdued young man merely stated, "I know what I saw, sir."

"Make it easier on yourself by coming quietly, now, sir," the constable advised as he then came toward the markedly shaken shopkeeper.

Before he could reach him, however, Mr Locke stepped into his path and said, "Pardon the intrusion, Constable—?"

"Groats."

"Constable Groats." Mr Locke gave a weak smile. "How delightful. Far be it for me to tell you how to perform your duty, but I do believe you would do well to hear what my wife and I have to say on the matter."

"And you are?"

"Percival Locke and Doctor Lynette Locke. We have been commissioned by Mr Foggity, in our capacities as members of the Bow Street Society, to discover the possible cause of his sudden decrease in height. After carefully considering all the facts, and gathering the necessary evidence, we are now able to give a logical explanation to his predicament."

"He's gone *mad,* that's what's happened," Mrs Foggity interjected, her voice now more angry than frightened. Everyone in the room turned toward her but it was the constable who spoke first.

"I want to hear what they've got to say. If I'm not satisfied with their explanation, then I'll arrest your husband."

"But he *struck* me!"

"All in good time, Mrs Foggity," Dr Locke remarked. Amy scowled at the alleged medicine woman but didn't speak further. Seeing she was pacified, at least for the time being, Constable Groats allowed Mr Locke to lead him to the shelving behind the counter.

"See these?" Mr Locke indicated some scratches in the right-hand wall of the wooden box and two small, round holes, one atop the other, underneath the top shelf. He explained, "This shelf has been moved upward recently. This hole is where the nail supporting the shelf used to be prior to being removed and repositioned the first time. This other is where the nail was removed and repositioned the second time. Mr Foggity told my wife and I that he had trouble reaching this topmost shelf where, previously, he had had no such problems. He then related to us how, just *two* days later, he was unable to reach this same shelf without the aid of a stool. He, as his wife has already stated, believes he rapidly decreased in height over the course of those two days. This evidence of the shelf having been moved twice, however, would suggest an external, and far more sinister, influence is at work here."

"You didn't move the shelf?" Constable Groats enquired Mr Foggity, to which the shopkeeper replied in the negative.

Mr Locke, who had to resist the urge to roll his eyes, said, "If he had been the one to move this shelf, Constable, he would not have come to the headquarters of the Bow Street Society in a state of such great agitation and fear."

"He could've forgotten he'd done it," Constable Groats pointed out.

Mr Locke hummed, "A plausible possibility, if this was the only thing which had given him cause to doubt his physical state. If you would be so good as to follow me." Locke moved around the policeman and into the kitchen. Groats duly obliged with the others following.

Once they were all gathered, Mr Locke picked up the chair from the left-hand side of the table, turned the chair onto its side, and laid it on the table's top. Doing the same with the chair on the right-hand side, he next pointed a slender finger at a leg on one chair and then on the other.

When Constable Groats bent over to peer at the two, Mr Locke said, "Mark the difference between the two, Constable. On this chair," Mr Locke indicated the one from the right-hand side, "the leg is solid. Yet, on the other chair's leg," he indicated the one from the left-hand side, "there is a distinct line where an addition has been made. If you will examine the remaining three legs on this chair, you will notice they have had the same treatment." Mr Locke and the constable simultaneously straightened.

The former, pointing downward, added, "And so, too, have the legs on the table itself and the legs of the third chair." Groats bent over for a second time, along with Mr Foggity, and said, "Cor, blimey, look at that!"

"Please confirm to the room, Mr Foggity, that your preferred choice of seat at breakfast is the one usually positioned on the right-hand side," Mr Locke enquired. Stunned, the shopkeeper could only nod. Mr Locke smiled, "By making the additions to the table and two of the chairs, someone has increased their height to create the illusion Mr Foggity's chair has shrunk."

"And you, Mrs Foggity," Dr Locke began. "Please confirm you have had your shoes altered to increase their height by showing them to the room."

"Don't be *silly*!" Mrs Foggity replied, giving a weak chuckle. When everyone remained silent however, and watched her with expectant eyes, her smile faded. She growled, "Why would I do that? I'm the one who keeps telling him he's not shrinking."

"Because you wish him to consider himself mad," Dr Locke retorted. "Or, at the very least, convince others he is thus so you may have him committed to Bedlam."

"Your earlier demands for his arrest, and insistence of his madness, are proof of that." Mr Locke said. "You did not act alone, however."

His gaze shifted to Mr Huddleston who at once

pointed to Mrs Foggity, and yelled, "It was all Mrs Foggity's idea, sir!"

"I have no doubt about it," Mr Locke replied. "She certainly seems to be a domineering woman. I knew you had played a part in it, though, when Mr Foggity informed me your late father was a carpenter by trade and had taught you all he knew. Only one skilled in the manipulation of wood could alter the table, chairs, and those shelves in such a way as to make the changes practically unnoticeable to the untrained eye. I assume you substituted the taller jars on the top shelf for marginally smaller, and wider, ones to further hide that the shelf had been lifted upward an inch."

Mr Huddleston gave a small nod but then bowed his head, shame evident upon his downcast features. Foggity, who had remained silent thus far, finally found his voice. He enquired, "But *why* would you want to do such a *horrible* thing to me, Godfrey?" He looked to his wife, "Amy?"

"I'd rather have rid of you than have to put up with you," Mrs Foggity snapped. "I'd never known such a boring, uninspiring, cowardly, unimpressive man existed until I married you. This shop could be thriving if you would only step out of your routine, but you weren't willing to do that. Godfrey was and I knew, between us, we could make this business as successful as those confectioners up north we read about in the 'papers. I knew you wouldn't give the business to him though, so we had to be rid of you another way." She turned to Groats, "No harm's been done though, has it? Not like we tried to do away with him."

"That'll be for a magistrate to decide," the constable replied and took hold of both Mrs Foggity and Mr Huddleston.

"One moment, Constable Groats," Dr Locke said, staying him. Holding out her handkerchief to Mrs Foggity, she added, "You may want to wipe the boot polish from your eye first." The other woman humphed and, tugging her arm free from Groats, used her sleeve to rub away the polish as she marched from the shop.

The Case of the Winchester Wife

I

"It's preposterous, expecting a man to unburden himself to a woman," Captain Bennett Winchester slurred as the mantel clock chimed. Though it was midmorning the Bow Street Society's parlour had neither daylight nor gaslight to soften the retired captain's pointed profile. Bloodshot, brown eyes looked beyond the wall as he approached, turned, and retraced his route, each thump of his boot succeeded by the heavy thud of his peg-leg.

Miss Trent's gaze tracked him during each pass of her armchair yet she remained seated. "Captain Winchester," she began, "you weren't obligated to come here and I wasn't obligated to receive you, yet here we are. Putting aside my disinclination to beg your pardon for my gender, I instead ask you to observe your surroundings. You and I are the only ones here. Therefore, your choice is clear—either swallow your masculine pride and tell me why you're here, or leave and put your trust in those at Bow Street Police Station."

"Don't speak such impertinence to *me*!" Captain Winchester barked, drawing Miss Trent to her feet.

She countered, "I shall speak whatever I want, Captain, when you are in *my* domain." His lips repeatedly furled and unfurled against gritted teeth while calloused hands, which had previously rested within his greatcoat's deep pockets, balled at his sides. Starting at his neck, his already pink face steadily flushed as if port had spilt under his skin.

He snarled, "How *daare* you, you uncouth *wretch.*"

"Continue as you are, Captain Winchester, and *I* will be calling upon the officers at Bow Street," Miss Trent promised despite his stale-rum-drenched breath turning her stomach. Whether it was the tone of her voice, her fixed gaze, the words themselves, or a combination of all three which cooled Captain Winchester's rage was unclear. Regardless the result was the same. After some aggressive chewing of his anger, the captain plonked himself in the vacant armchair. Miss Trent wasn't naïve enough to think it ended, however. Instead, she enabled additional calming time by fetching tea from the kitchen. Coffee would've been more sobering for him but, alas, she suspected such a blatant assumption wouldn't have been welcomed by his volatile temper.

In due course Captain Winchester's pallid complexion had returned and his hands had come to rest upon his thighs. She poured the amber liquid in silence and he accepted the cup without remark. "I must beg your pardon for my brutishness, Miss Trent," he muttered against the steam rising from his cup. Taking a second sip, he balanced it on its saucer and put both down while continuing, "I would say it was the worry for my wife which drove my temper but that would be a plain dishonesty." Miss Trent held her tongue as the truth of his words hung between them like a lead weight. "I'm not aggrieved by your silence, Miss Trent." He withdrew against the armchair's back corner and the elongated shadows cast by its wings seemed to age him beyond his forty years.

"I came to London to work," his sombre voice began from the depths. "I was offered the position of ship's captain on a trading vessel bound for Scotland. The company had heard of my reputation for being a loyal employee who wouldn't permit the allure of illicit profit to compromise his integrity." The fingers of Captain Winchester's right hand strummed his knee, mere inches above his wooden appendage. "And they weren't perturbed by my affliction when I informed them of it in my letters." He paused to allow the expression of disgust or sympathy that usually followed such a statement. Yet all he received was stoicism masked by a curt nod and a sip of tea.

His Adam's apple constricted and his jaw began to

clench. "*This* morning, *then*," he resumed as his fingers curled. "My wife, Daphne, and I travelled by railway from Liverpool to London's King's Cross. The company had arranged for us to be *met*, by private carriage, at the railway station to take Daphne to our new residence and *me* to the company's offices. As expected, when the two of us left the station, we were met by their driver. He, alongside myself and the station's porter, loaded our few trunks and boxes onto the carriage's roof. My wife, in the meantime, waited at the station door. The bustling crowd, the dirt in the air, and the traffic moving every which way compelled her to alight the carriage soon after." Captain Winchester's voice had quickened the more he'd realised how little emotion Miss Trent expressed. "There were carriages on three sides, boxing ours in. Daphne wanted to leave."

"Did she tell you that?"

"No, of *course* not!" he snapped. "*She* never made such a *spectacle* in public. Being her husband, I *knew* she was getting agitated." He made a flourish with his hand, "She was looking behind our carriage and in front. In the end, I told her to get in and close the curtains."

"And did she?"

"Are you *trying* my patience on *purpose*—?" He abruptly interrupted himself and stood. Though he towered over her, Miss Trent felt no fear. She didn't hide this fact, either.

Standing to look him in the eye, she said, "Your wife climbed into the carriage and closed its curtains. What then?"

"She *disappeared*," Captain Winchester growled.

At once, Miss Trent enquired, "She left the carriage?"

"*No,* she *disappeared.* She *closed* the door, *drew* the curtains, and was inside, *alone,* for mere *seconds,* before I *opened* the door and found the carriage *empty*!"

II

After listening to Captain Winchester's tale, Mr Samuel Snyder sat back and scratched a bushy side-burn with his fat finger. In his rough, East-End-of-London accented voice, he said, "That does sound peculiar." With larger-than-average hands, broad arms, and even broader shoulders, Mr Snyder wasn't feeble. This, coupled with the great cloak and shallow, wide-brimmed hat he'd discarded upon arrival, were evidence of the years spent driving a two-wheeler Hansom cab. Brown, beady eyes, set deeply in Mr Snyder's weathered face, regarded Captain Winchester with sympathy as Mr Snyder enquired, "You said this woz outside King's Cross?"

"*Yes*, this morning," Captain Winchester replied but was immediately distracted by Miss Georgina Dexter softly clearing her throat. Miss Dexter was shorter than Mr Snyder at only five feet—he was a good six inches taller— but her petite form was nevertheless perfectly proportioned. At eighteen years old, Miss Dexter enjoyed the beauty afforded by youth; her fair skin was flawless, while the red of her hair was striking in its darker shade. She'd chosen a light brown, straight-lined skirt this day. Above it she wore a matching, waist-long jacket whose sleeves adhered to the fashionable mutton-chop shape. Its double lapels were dark-brown on the bottom and a matching colour to the jacket on top. Beneath, she wore a high-necked, plain-white blouse with frilled collar. A small, round, silver brooch was pinned to the centre of the high neck, with no other adornments. Her hair was brushed back and pinned into an understated, practical plait running the length of her head and nestled within the nape of her neck.

Miss Dexter lowered her gaze the instant Captain Winchester glowered her way. Her pencil, poised over the sketchbook in her lap, had yet to make a mark. Mr Snyder leant forward, so as to shield Miss Dexter from view, and said, "Busy station that, what with *Great Northern* trains going from there up to York and ending there on the way back. What did the carriage she got into look like?"

"Black with four wheels and two horses," Captain Winchester replied.

Mr Snyder enquired, "And what was on the door?" Without giving their client a moment to answer though he straightened and, addressing Miss Dexter, added, "Draw this, please, Miss Dexter?"

"It didn't *have* anything on its door," Captain Winchester interrupted, his hand once again forming a ball upon his thigh.

Mr Snyder turned his head and, with a knitted brow, enquired, "Didn't have anything, Captain? *Nothing* at all? Not even the company's name?"

"That's what I *said,* isn't it?" Captain Winchester growled.

Yet Mr Snyder simply enquired, "Wasn't that a bit peculiar to you, Captain?"

"*No,* and this *damnable* farce is wasting time!" Captain Winchester yelled, simultaneously standing. His sweat-covered forehead glistened in the lamplight as he paced the room without care for the racket caused by his peg-leg. Both Mr Snyder and Miss Dexter watched his progress for a few moments, but it was the former who eventually rose from his chair to block his path.

He said, "We can't find your wife if we don't know where to look. The company that wrote you is who sent the carriage but there wasn't anything for you to know it woz the right one, bar what the driver told you. The carriage and driver are what we've got to find first as they might know where your wife went.

"Now, if she was nabbed from the carriage, she would've yelled or the ones nabbing her would've yelled, or both. You would've seen their feet or them running off, too. King's Cross is a busy station and there's lots of carriages and the like there," Mr Snyder scratched his cheek and continued, "You said there woz carriages boxing yours in. Means no one could get to your wife from the other side, if they woz walking, without anyone seeing them. What woz the name of the company who got you to London, Captain?"

"*Phoenix & Dove*," Captain Winchester replied, gifting Mr Snyder with the same stale-rum-drenched breath as earlier. Mr Snyder didn't flinch, however. Instead he waited as the seaman pulled some folded paper from his greatcoat's inside pocket and gave it to him. While Mr Snyder read over the four lines of text typed onto the paper, Captain Winchester explained, "This was the letter I received from them." Though short the correspondence did in fact invite Captain Bennett Winchester (Retired) and his wife, Mrs Daphne Winchester, to London for the former to captain a merchant vessel, called *The White Dove*, on its maiden voyage to Scotland.

Miss Dexter's meek voice suddenly enquired, "*The* letter, Captain Winchester? Were there no others?"

"*Should* there have been?" Captain Winchester challenged but then discarded his gaze upon Miss Dexter in favour of Mr Snyder. He said, "The company's address is at the top."

"St. Katherine's Docks?" Mr Snyder clarified with a second knitting of his brow. Captain Winchester chewed his tongue as the port-colour seeped from his neck upwards.

He growled, "I've given you *everything* I know in this matter. *Get* yourselves from *here* and *find* my *wife*!"

"You haven't described her to us, though," Miss Dexter pointed out as, with sketchbook clutched to her chest, she approached. The scowl Captain Winchester tossed toward her gave her cause to hesitate but not abandon her task. "Should you do so, I may sketch her likeness. Mr Snyder and I may then show it to those who are employed at King's Cross and any who visit it daily."

"Don't you think that was the *first* thing I *did*?" Captain Winchester sneered.

Miss Dexter swallowed but didn't break her gaze

with their client. Instead she replied, "I'm certain of it, Captain, but, as Mr Snyder has said, King's Cross is a busy station with trains going from and to York in the north. There may be passengers returning this afternoon that departed this morning and saw your wife."

Captain Winchester stopped chewing and, after considering the idea, lost the spilt port colour from his features. Nevertheless, it was with great reluctance that he agreed by saying, "She's half-caste, olive-skinned. Her mother was African-French, her father American. It makes her *very* vulnerable to the ignorance-fuelled hatred of others. She's taken to wearing a white, lace veil and cotton gloves to hide her caste because of it. If *I* had my way, they'd get a musket ball to the *head*."

"Does she ever remove her veil?" Miss Dexter enquired and lowered herself into the nearest armchair.

Captain Winchester rolled his tongue about his closed mouth and answered, "Only when I'm on hand to prevent such attacks with my presence."

Miss Dexter hummed and enquired, "Should she remove it though, what are the colour of her eyes, the shape of her nose, and the size of her mouth? Does she have any scars, moles, birthmarks, or unusual features which may be memorable to others?"

"Her eyes are brown and large," Captain Winchester replied, stifling a sigh. "She's twenty-two years old, has a large nose, large mouth, no scars, no moles, and no birthmarks." He suddenly turned and, striding to the door, added, "Send word once you've found her but, until then, *get* on with what I'll be *paying* you for and *leave* me be."

Mr Snyder and Miss Dexter had watched his abrupt retreat but neither attempted to prevent his departure. It was only when the outer door slammed that Mr Snyder followed, the letter clutched in his large hand. "If this is where I think it is then we've gotta get there as fast as Red-Shirt will take us."

"Why?" Miss Dexter enquired as she closed her

sketchbook and joined him at the parlour door. Mr Snyder stuffed the letter into his pocket and, stepping into the hallway, replied, "Because there's no company called that there."

III

The sun struggled to break through dense clouds as Mr Snyder's two-wheeler cab arrived at the gates to St. Katherine's Docks. The usual sights of ships being unloaded and loaded met the two Bow Streeters as they continued their journey on foot. Fortunately, the crowds of men were too absorbed by their work to take notice of two strangers walking among them along the quayside toward the warehouses. During their last case together, Mr Snyder and Miss Dexter had learnt strangers were commonplace at the docks. They were never questioned about their origins, their name, or social class. Provided they carried out the work to the Quay-Gangers' satisfaction, they were left alone. Women at the quayside were more noticeable but Mr Snyder was careful to shield Miss Dexter with his body.

The group of warehouses they looked for stood like watchmen along the waterfront. Each one was a hub of activity with many workers entering and leaving as cargo from the ships was stored and cargo to be shipped was removed. The Bow Streeters weaved their way through the chaos until they reached the last warehouse in the row. Set apart from the others, not only by its physical distance, but also its state of disrepair, this warehouse was eerily quiet. Miss Dexter looked up at the desolate structure, her hand pinning her bonnet against the wind. "Are we here, Sam?"

"We are." Mr Snyder approached a window to peer through one of its many broken panes. Beyond was a vast, empty space shrouded in darkness. After a while his eyes had adjusted enough to enable him to see a couple of crates standing in its middle, however. Between them were some blankets laid out upon the ground and a carpet bag.

"Sam!" Miss Dexter shrieked, compelling him to turn his head—just in time to see a fist hurtling toward him. Mr Snyder ducked and a remaining pane above his head smashed, dusting him with glass. A cry also sounded, followed by a dragging of feet. Taking his chance, Mr Snyder swerved to the right while standing at the same time. Immediately turning on the spot and lifting his clenched fists in defence, Mr Snyder came face-to-face with a brown-eyed, olive-skinned male grasping his bleeding knuckles. In a heartbeat, this same male then lunged forward with his other fist held aloft. Mr Snyder retaliated by driving his own hefty hand into the side of the male's head and, while he was dazed, shoving him against the warehouse wall. The weight of Mr Snyder's hand against his chest met the male's subsequent attempt to break free.

Mr Snyder, whose voice was made all the rougher by the exertion, enquired, "Who are you and what're you doing trying to clobber me?" The man, who couldn't have been any older than twenty, pursed his lips. Mr Snyder grunted as he jerked his arms upwards to lift him from the ground.

The man's eyes widened and he cried, "Michael! My name's Michael!"

"You're a long way from home, Michael," Mr Snyder remarked when he heard his accent, unsure if it was American or Canadian, as he'd only ever heard Doctor Weeks talking. He added, "I'm Sam Snyder and that's Miss Georgina Dexter. We're from the Bow Street Society and you've still not told me why you woz trying to hit me."

"I had to get you before you got me, didn't I?" Michael answered.

Mr Snyder's face scrunched up with anger, however, as he countered, "I was looking through the bloody window, mate."

"Yeah, looking for me," Michael said, "for Captain Winchester, yeah?"

"What do you know about Captain Winchester?" Mr Snyder challenged.

"Nothing," Michael replied but Mr Snyder wasn't convinced. He tightened his grip upon Michael's shirt until he felt the weight of his knuckles pressing against his Adam's apple. Michael's breath caught in his throat and he cried, "I was his driver!" Michael's uninjured fingers attempted to prise Mr Snyder's from him but he wasn't strong enough. He went on, "When his woman disappeared this morning. He was angry—the angriest I've ever seen a fella! I was sure he blamed me for it—now you've come to do me in!"

"Don't be foolish, boy. The Society's against violence," Mr Snyder retorted and put Michael down. Taking hold of the lad's arm, he tied his own handkerchief tightly around Michael's bleeding knuckles. "You okay?" Mr Snyder enquired from Miss Dexter, keeping a hand on Michael's shoulder.

Miss Dexter offered a weak smile but replied, "Yes, thank you, Sam." The two simultaneously returned their gazes to Michael as Miss Dexter enquired, "The company who invited Captain Winchester to London, *Phoenix & Dove*, gave their address as this warehouse. Did they give you the same?"

"Yeah," Michael replied though his answer lacked conviction. Glancing at the warehouse over his shoulder, he said, "Was given the carriage, told where to drive it to, and where to take it after—never knew the fella's name that gave me the work."

"Have you drove carriages before?" Mr Snyder enquired to which Michael replied in the negative. "How'd you come to get the work, then?" Mr Snyder moved closer and, catching Michael's second glance at the warehouse, pointed at it. Mr Snyder enquired, "Want to show me what's in there?"

"Nothing," Michael countered. "I was asked by a fella if I could drive and I told him yeah. I needed the cash. I've not done anything; I didn't see Daphne get out of the carriage or see anyone get in. I did the work and got the pay, that's all."

"Woz the carriage took back here?" Mr Snyder enquired. Michael sidestepped to bar the only door on that side of the warehouse.

He replied, "*No,* I *told* you; there's *nothing* in there. Why don't you ask Captain Winchester where his wife's gone? He was the one yelling at her, treating her worse than a dog."

"So you think she could've run away, then?" Miss Dexter ventured.

Michael nodded, saying, "Makes sense, doesn't it? Someone as good as her shouldn't have to put up with someone as bad as him."

"You know a lot about it for a bloke who just done some driving for them," Mr Snyder remarked, causing Michael to hesitate before he replied.

"Well, it was obvious, wasn't it? I got the stink of rum from him as soon as he come near. Then he was barking orders at her, telling her to get out of the way then telling her to get in the carriage. If she wanted away from him, then no one who knew her would judge her for it." Michael reached behind him and opened the door. He added, "And would be cruel to throw her back to a fella like him, too, if you ask me. You can tell him I said that."

"And what surname should I give when I do?" Mr Snyder enquired.

Michael shook his head though and said, "Nah, you're not getting that from me." Without waiting for their reaction, Michael slipped into the warehouse, letting the door swing shut behind him, and hurried to the crates.

Mr Snyder remarked, "He knows more than what he's telling us." The moment Mr Snyder opened the door though, Michael ran. He snatched up the suitcase and vanished in the shadows. Mr Snyder had already given chase, but the sound of a second door slamming brought him to an abrupt stop.

Spinning around, he ran back to Miss Dexter and yelled, "Outside!" Having already put one foot inside, Miss Dexter at once removed it to hop aside and give Mr Snyder enough room to run past and along the row of warehouses. She hitched her skirts and did her level best to keep pace with her friend. Skirts and high winds don't mix, however, and Miss Dexter was a few seconds behind Mr Snyder when he stopped at the row's end.

"Where is—?" she began but her words were lost to the wind as a four-wheeled, two-horse, black carriage sped out from behind the warehouses into the throng of dock workers. Many of whom had to dive into the water to avoid being run down. At the vehicle's helm was Michael, while a passenger darted from the window upon catching sight of Mr Snyder and Miss Dexter looking their way. It was too late, however. For, despite the carriage's tremendous speed, there had been no mistaking the white, lace veil and cotton gloves…

IV

"Miss Dexter and me went to King's Cross on the way back and took a look. There woz enough room there for two four-wheeler carriages to sit side by side when the luggage woz loaded," Mr Snyder explained. Outside, the day was on the cusp of dusk; the indistinct clouds had turned the sky an ashen grey, made lighter by the newly setting sun behind. It was not yet dark enough to light the lamps, however. Nor the hearths; the humidity that had plagued London all day long still retained its grip, making the parlour feel decidedly muggy.

Nonetheless, Miss Trent and Miss Dexter each held their focus as Mr Snyder held one horizontal hand in front of the other and continued, "Let's say this is Captain Winchester's carriage." He gave a small jerk of his front hand. "My fingers are the horses." Mr Snyder repeated the gesture with his back hand. "And this is the second with the horses facing the other way. Four-wheeler carriages have big doors that open outwards. I should know. I've had many near misses with 'em when driving the cab. Anyway, they also got a step to help people climb in and out of them. Well, what I think happened is this. After Mrs Winchester had got in her carriage, closed the door on the station side, and closed the curtain, she then opened the door on the road side. This other carriage, with *its* door open, too, would've hid her moving between them. The steps on both would've helped her get across as well."

"Wouldn't the carriages have rocked as she left one and entered the other?" Miss Trent enquired.

Mr Snyder smiled and said, "Yeah, which is why she had to have had help."

"The driver. Michael," Miss Dexter interjected with a smile. "Mr Snyder thinks both drivers were working for Mrs Winchester and I'm inclined to agree. Michael certainly spoke far more intimately about Mrs Winchester than he ought to've as a stranger. He even referred to her by her first name."

"It woz probably him that sent the letter to Captain Winchester to get him down here from Liverpool in the first place," Mr Snyder said. "Someone would've had to have told him about Captain Winchester's past work as a merchant seaman. Mrs Winchester could've told him that."

"The fictitious company's name is also telling of Mrs Winchester's plan. *Phoenix & Dove.* The phoenix is a bird that rose from the ashes to be born again and the dove is a bird sent by Noah from the ark to find land," Miss Dexter explained. "Each brought about a new beginning after wretchedness, the same thing Mrs Winchester must've hoped for by escaping her brutish husband."

"The passenger you saw inside Michael's carriage wore a veil though," Miss Trent pointed out. She added, "It could've been anyone."

"Nah," Mr Snyder said with a shake of his head. "Michael woz desperate enough to try and clobber me, so we wouldn't go in the warehouse. He thought we woz there for Captain Winchester. I think they woz planning on hiding there a while but, when we got there, they decided to scarper."

"And the other driver?" Miss Trent enquired. The Bow Streeters exchanged glances but it was Miss Dexter who replied.

"There wasn't a third person, either on or in Michael's carriage when he passed us. Also, as Captain Winchester didn't remark upon another carriage being behind his own while at King's Cross, it's unlikely he saw either it or whoever drove it."

"Your drawing of Mrs Winchester, Miss Dexter," Miss Trent began before asking, "Is it likely anyone could recognise her if we were to place it in the *Gaslight Gazette*?" Miss Dexter opened her sketchbook at the relevant page, but nonetheless shook her head.

She replied, "Captain Winchester's description was rather vague. Her reluctance to forego her veil while in the presumed safety of Michael's carriage also suggests she intends to continue wearing it. It's unlikely then that anyone, who may see the sketch in the newspaper, would be given the chance to see her face."

"So, we have no way of identifying Mrs Winchester's current location or where she may be going," Miss Trent stated.

"America, I would say," Mr Snyder replied and rested his hands upon his belly. He added, "Can't say for sure, but Michael could've been a brother or cousin, what with him and Mrs Winchester being close in age and both being from over there."

"Is my being glad we failed to find her a terrible thing, Miss Trent?" Miss Dexter enquired, her naturally meek voice made all the meeker by its forced quietness.

Her face blossomed into a smile though when Miss Trent replied, "Far from it, for I'm glad, too. It means I shan't have to lie to Captain Winchester. Fortunately, he's not paid us a penny so that'll make delivering the news easier."

"What about the Society's reputation?" Mr Snyder enquired.

Miss Trent's brow lofted as she replied, "Sam, some things in this life are more important than reputation."

The Case of the Perilous Pet

I

Smoke billowed from a pipe's bowl as pale lips repeatedly puckered and relaxed around its bit. Having imbibed enough to satisfy his craving, the pipe's owner lowered and held it in his wrinkled, emaciated hand upon his lean knee. A clattering of china attracted his pale-green eyes to a tea tray placed onto a low table before him. The bearer, a young woman of twenty-eight years, took a seat on a tête-à-tête sofa to his armchair's left, facing a cold hearth.

Both pieces of furniture were upholstered in a navy-blue fabric, embroidered with light-blue leaves to complement the primary colour of the bronze gilt paper adorning the parlour's walls. The aforementioned table matched the fireplace's ornately carved surround in that it, too, was made from oak. Its Queen Anne feet stood on a square rug laid over exposed—yet polished—floorboards. The rug's light blue-and-cream leaves, set against a dark-blue background, perfectly complemented its surrounds.

Beneath a moustache of brilliant white, the pipe owner's tongue snaked across his lips as he laid eyes upon the Victoria sponge cake in the tray's centre.

"How do you take your tea, Mr Treaves?" his hostess enquired.

"Cream with one, please," he replied, lifting his gaze to meet hers. "Did… you bake the cake, Miss Trent?"

"Yes, would you like some?" she offered.

Mr Treaves hummed, nodding as he put down his pipe in readiness. Miss Rebecca Trent, after completing the preparation of his tea, set it down on his side of the table. She next reached for the cake slice and cut into the light sponge.

"So, how may the Bow Street Society be of assistance?" she enquired once he'd accepted the plated-up cake with his free hand. Emaciated hands and white facial hair aside, his sixty-odd years could be perceived in his rounded shoulders and dark blotches littering his skin. A skin so thin the Society's clerk could follow the contours of his cheekbones and knuckles without scrutiny.

His preferred choice of attire, a thigh-length coat with skirt—more commonly known as a frock coat—over a black suit with matching waistcoat, hinted at a more conservative world view. The only signs of his current financial health were the chain of a gold pocket watch draped across one half of his waistcoat and some gold cufflinks in his shirt's sleeves. He'd arrived with an ebony walking cane, topped with a silver ball handle, which he'd left in the hall alongside his ankle-length, black fur coat, top hat, and scarf. These latter two accompaniments had evidenced, in Miss Trent's mind, a stronger vulnerability to the cold. Especially since the day hadn't only contained plentiful sunshine but also high humidity.

She had chosen a much lighter material in lieu of this fact. Her bustle dress was therefore pale-yellow cotton with white lace on its three-quarter-length sleeves and high, square collar. To further lessen the chances of overheating, she'd pinned up her chestnut-brown hair to expose her neck. Her fair complexion also lacked its usual blusher for it would've likely run the moment she'd started sweating.

"For over thirty years, I've been retained by Sir Thomas Russell as his solicitor," Mr Treaves began, when he'd savoured a morsel of cake. "Delicious," he added with a smile. Switching the cake for his tea, he continued, "We'd also become good friends during that time." He took a quiet slurp and replaced the cup upon its saucer. "As you can imagine, then, it came as quite the shock to receive news of his sudden passing."

Miss Trent's hand, lifting her own teacup, halted. Meeting his gaze with a loft of her brow, she replied, "Indeed."

"It was a month ago now," Mr Treaves went on.

Miss Trent, having taken her intended sip, put down her drink to commence taking short-hand notes of the discussion. Waiting a moment, Mr Treaves said, "Mr Appleby, Sir Russell's manservant, found him on the floor at the foot of the stairs. He'd heard a cry and the sound of something heavy tumbling down them. It took only a few moments to reach him but, by the time Mr Appleby had, Sir Russell was dead—his neck broken."

"Was a doctor called?"

"Yes. He confirmed the cause of death. He explained a younger man may have survived the fall, but Sir Russell's frail bones had sealed his fate. Eighty years old, he was. Much older than I or even Mr Appleby." Mr Treaves frowned. "Doctor said he wouldn't have felt a thing—even after his neck had snapped. A small mercy." Another morsel of cake, clasped between thumb and forefinger, was deposited into his mouth. Smacking his lips together as he sucked—not chewed—the sponge, he added, "One reads about heads still showing life after being cut from the body. Speaking, blushing, and the like."

"There was no question it was an accident?" Miss Trent enquired to sharpen his focus.

Swallowing, Mr Treaves shook his head and had another slurp of tea. "None at all. Not in my mind, Mr Appleby's, the doctor's, or even the coroner's. Sir Russell's son, Stephen, was a different matter entirely, however." The solicitor gathered up the remaining crumbs and, still gripping them, slipped both thumb and forefinger into his mouth to their knuckles.

"He has accused Sir Russell's Staffordshire bull terrier of murder," Mr Treaves added, putting the plate down.

"Pardon?" she enquired, halting, this time in her writing, to stare at him.

"Stephen's argument rests on the well-known fact Claude followed Sir Russell everywhere. The younger Russell insists the dog must have crossed his father's path while he was descending the stairs—thus causing Sir Russell to catch his foot and tumble down the stairs to his death."

"Did Stephen see his father fall?"

"No, no one did. Master Russell hasn't resided in his father's home for years and Mr Appleby was in another part of the house altogether. There's a cook and butler, of course, but they were tending to their duties elsewhere."

"Why is Master Russell convinced it was Claude, then, if the coroner has already ruled Sir Russell's death an accident?"

"Because, Miss Trent, he is determined to prove Claude guilty to disinherit him," Mr Treaves stated. Miss Trent must have looked the very picture of confusion for he at once continued, "Other than a small legacy for Mr Appleby and a sum to settle my fee as executor, Sir Russell's will bequeathed the entirety of his estate to his dog."

"*Pardon*?" Miss Trent's eyes widened. "But surely a *dog* can't legally inherit?"

"It can when the terms of the will stipulate the monies are to be used to ensure the dog's wellbeing and comfort, as Sir Russell's did." Mr Treaves drank his last drop of tea and dabbed at the corners of his mouth with his handkerchief. "I knew of the will's contents, of course, because I'd advised Sir Russell on its legality. His son didn't, however. When the will was read therefore, he erupted into a rage and vowed to see to the dog's destruction. That is when he made his ridiculous allegation."

"Do you have any idea why Sir Russell would disinherit his son?"

"Stephen has a penchant for the gambling tables and assembly rooms. His father believed, as do I, the family fortune would be squandered within a matter of months—if not weeks—should Stephen be given access to it."

"Would he be? If Claude's guilt was proven and he was destroyed?"

"Unfortunately, yes," Mr Treaves replied. "Currently, it's Stephen's word against Mr Appleby's, but

I wouldn't think it beneath Stephen to fabricate evidence to serve his purpose. To answer your earlier question about how the Bow Street Society may assist me, Miss Trent, I need it to conduct an independent investigation into Sir Russell's death and prove, once and for all, the truth of the matter. Should evidence be found to substantiate Stephen's allegation, I would, as the will's executor, grant Master Russell access to his father's estate. If, on the other hand, Claude is proven innocent, I shall have incontestable grounds on which to carry out Sir Russell's final wishes."

"I understand," Miss Trent replied in a sombre tone. "The Society accepts your commission, Mr Treaves. If you could give me the address of Sir Russell's residence, I will make arrangements for two of our members to meet you there today."

"Yes, of course. Thank you, Miss Trent." Mr Treaves smiled. "May I have another slice of cake?"

II

A two-wheeler hansom cab trundled along a dirt road, the uneven surface of which causing the cab to bounce and bump its occupants. Only the cab's heavy doors, closed over their knees, prevented the two men from being thrown onto the horse's hind legs. Approximately four feet wide and made of wood with a metal rim, the wheels were better suited to the manure-strewn cobbled streets of London. So, too, was its driver—Mr Samuel Snyder. Sitting upon a raised seat at the back of the cab, he had a clear view across its top. The reins, manipulated by his large, calloused hands, ran across the cab's roof, through an upside-down 'Y' attachment, and down to the horse's harness. The main body of the cab consisted of a large, wooden box, closed on three sides, resting on the wheels' axle. The previously described doors were fixed, by hinges, to the left and right sides, on a slant. This, coupled with the point in the doors' centre, ensured passengers' knees could be accommodated once they sat, side by side, on the narrow, leather-upholstered bench. Glassless windows in the sides of the cab, in addition to the open front, allowed air to circulate around its occupants. On this particularly humid day, the two men housed within the cab were most grateful for this.

"Cherry Drop, Dr Alexander?" one offered the other as an open, brown paper bag emerged from beneath the doors. Though in his mid-twenties, the bag-holding man's unblemished complexion, smooth jaw, soft, light-brown hair, and large eyes alluded to a much younger age. His overall boyish appearance was enhanced further by the unusually wide, starched Eaton collar he wore. For not only did it hide his entire neck, it created the illusion of his head being much smaller than it actually was. Thus, when one looked to his clothes—a dark-brown, three-piece suit, white shirt, and brown tie flecked with gold—one inevitably suspected he'd borrowed his father's Sunday best.

"Ah, thank you very much, Mr Heath," Dr Rupert Alexander replied with a hint of an Edinburgh accent.

At thirty-seven, he was considerably older than his fellow Bow Streeter. Unlike Mr Heath, who wore a bowler hat, Dr Alexander's wavy, short, black hair—parted at the side—was uncovered. Straight, thick, black brows capped his chestnut-brown eyes, while his most distinguishing features were his large, jutting-out ears and pointed nose. For some, these latter elements may have defined Dr Alexander as ugly. When regarded with his brows, eyes, and strong, clean-shaven jaw, however, they made him very handsome indeed. His attire was just as admirable; a fastened, double-breasted, dark-grey, cotton jacket over a cream-coloured shirt, with a plain, black bowtie and matching trousers. Retrieving a hard-boiled sweet from the bag, Dr Alexander popped it into his mouth.

The cab, which had turned off the dirt road, passed through a set of open, wrought-iron, spiked gates and journeyed along a narrow, gravel-covered driveway. Within moments, an expansive lawn, dotted with ancient oak trees, was all Mr Heath and Dr Alexander could see for miles on both sides. Ahead, the driveway seemed to disappear into a horizon of dark-green foliage.

Such was the sight from within the cab until, after almost ten minutes of travel, the driveway curved. As the cab followed its trajectory, the mass of green slid away and a grand house took its place. Set against the brilliant blue of the summer sky, and facing the sun, the house seemed to shimmer like gold. So resplendent was it, Mr Heath gasped and almost choked on his Cherry Drop. A few hard whacks on his back by Dr Alexander's hand, however, soon dislodged it.

"Th—thank you, Doctor," Mr Heath wheezed, depositing the bag into his inside pocket.

"You're welcome."

The cab drew nearer still to the residence, leaving the army of oak trees in its wake. From the closer vantage point, Mr Heath could distinguish two complete wings of the house. At a rough estimate, Mr Heath would say the entire residence contained a minimum of one hundred rooms. Straight, stone steps led from terraces on the left and right sides of the house's façade to converge in a lower, much longer terrace in the centre. From there, two more flights of steps, slanting away from the left and right terraces, led to the ground.

Framing the lower stairs were small, round windows—possibly those of the kitchen and male servants' quarters—while three sets of double, French doors lined the central terrace. Yet more doors opened out onto the left and right terraces. Six tall windows filled the spaces between the doors in the centre and those on the side terraces. Identical windows then lined the upper two levels. In the roof, Mr Heath saw much smaller windows—presumably the female servants' living space. Every window in the place had wooden frames painted a brilliant white, with many small, square panes.

A rectangle of gravel-strewn ground was sandwiched between the house and driveway's end. On reaching it, the cab took a swift left and completed a short, tight curve before slowing to a stop underneath the central terrace. Mr Heath and Dr Alexander, upon releasing its doors, climbed from the cab soon after.

Hearing the shuffling of feet from above, the two men looked up to see Mr Treaves' wrinkled face peering down at them from the terrace's stone ballasts. Another gentleman—also in his sixties but with a superficially more robust physique than Mr Treaves'—stepped into view beside the solicitor. He was attired in a knee-length brown coat over a black frock coat, trousers, cravat, and waistcoat. The white of his shirt could barely be seen under his many layers, only its collar and cuff edges. A neat, dark-grey beard framed his jaw and merged into the swept-back, dark-grey hair upon his head. His upper lip was clean shaven while minute tuffs of white hair protruded from his red, bulbous nose. He lifted a large hand to the newcomers.

"Good afternoon, gentlemen, and welcome to Russell Hall!" Mr Treaves called to them. Before either Mr Heath or Dr Alexander could respond, however, he'd disappeared from sight—along with his companion. The two Bow Streeters exchanged glances but remained where they stood when they heard their hosts descending the steps.

"I'm Mr Treaves, Sir Russell's solicitor, and this is his manservant, Mr Appleby," the solicitor introduced once they'd assembled.

"A pleasure to make your acquaintances, Mr Treaves, Mr Appleby," Dr Alexander replied. He shook their hands and, glancing at his travelling companion, continued, "This is Mr Bertram Heath, an architect and associate of the Royal Institute of British Architects. I'm Doctor Rupert Alexander, a veterinary surgeon and graduate of the Royal Veterinary College. Miss Trent has asked us to investigate the matter you came to our Society about, Mr Treaves."

"A very serious matter it is, too," Mr Appleby interjected with a curt nod.

"Indeed it is," Mr Treaves agreed. Turning toward the terrace, he added, "If you'd like to come this way, gentlemen, Mr Appleby and I will show you where Sir Russell fell."

"My expertise is in animal health and wellbeing, Mr Treaves," Dr Alexander replied. "I'd like to examine the Staffordshire bull terrier—build an overall picture of his physical capabilities and inhibitions."

"I *do* recall the mention of stairs in Miss Trent's letter," Mr Heath said. "They may hold the key to the matter, but it does depend upon their state of repair, design, depth of step—oh, *delightful*!" he exclaimed, having noticed the view once he'd joined the others on the terrace.

Turning to the house, he shaded his eyes with his hand and arched his back to admire the façade. Still in position, he remarked, "Eighteenth century neo-classicism, if I'm not mistaken. An exceedingly popular style during that time, and in the early years of our own century. It has always been one of my favourites. So grand, so impressive, so—"

"The stairs are this way, Mr Heath," Mr Treaves' voice interrupted from within.

"Oh, yes," Mr Heath replied, at once straightening. As he dropped his hand, he stepped through the open doorway, and joined the others.

"Claude is in Sir Russell's bedroom, Dr Alexander," Mr Treaves explained. "Mr Appleby will take you to him."

"Thank you," Dr Alexander smiled and, following the manservant, climbed a curved staircase to the first-floor landing. Carpeted with a rich, red covering, the staircase was one of two which followed the curves of the rounded reception hall. Mr Heath, having taken a tailor's tape measure from his pocket, meanwhile crouched beside the bottom step.

"May I ask what you're doing… Mr Heath?" Mr Treaves enquired as he came up behind him and peered over his shoulder.

"Measuring the depth of the steps, Mr Treaves, to help us decide if Sir Russell lost his balance due to their height."

"I see…" A short pause followed before Mr Treaves revealed, "But he didn't fall down these stairs." Both men rose at the same time and looked to a dark-oak door in the corner to which the solicitor pointed. Mr Treaves explained, "Sir Russell used the back stairs for the last two years." Mr Treaves and Mr Heath turned toward the carpeted stairs as the former added, "The curve of those gave him the feeling of being unbalanced."

"The incline is rather steep," Mr Heath remarked.

Mr Treaves hummed and, turning with a shuffle, walked to the indicated door. He said, "If you'll follow me, I'll show you the stairs he *did* fall down."

"Thank you," Mr Heath replied with a smile.

"Much obliged."

III

Dr Alexander and Mr Appleby stood in the corner of Sir Russell's bedchamber after stepping through its open doorway. To their direct right was a four-posted, English oak-framed bed. Depictions of berries, flowers, and leaves were carved into the bed's upper beams, while a dust-and-cobweb-covered, dark-purple canopy hung from a hook directly above. Pairs of heavy, damask curtains—folded and tied to the posts—ran along the beams' undersides, thus creating a barrier against the cold when drawn. Thick, square cabinets—as ornately carved as the beams and made of the same wood—stood on either side of the bed. Silver candlesticks, rather than kerosene lamps, were placed in the centre of these cabinets, complete with well-used candles. Beside each candlestick was a candle snuffer, silver, bell-shaped objects attached to long, ebony handles which had been turned during carving to provide a more comfortable grip.

To Dr Alexander and Mr Appleby's direct left were two, three-door armoires— also made of dark, English oak. On the wall facing the foot of the bed was a fireplace. Its carvings, etched into the stone framing the iron hearth, echoed those on the bed. The entirety of the fireplace certainly impressed Dr Alexander. The usual pokers, tongs, and brass bed warmer were arranged in racks on the plain base of the fire's surround. Mounted on the wall above the fireplace was an oil painting of a woman in her twenties. Golden haired, blue eyed, and slender in form, the woman sat looking out at the viewer with her bosom barely covered by material. She had a smile upon her face and a look in her eye, inviting the viewer to join her and remove the remainder of her coverings. Walking further into the bedchamber, Dr Alexander was drawn to the painting.

"Lady Abigail Russell," Mr Appleby said as he joined the Bow Streeter before the fireplace. "She passed while bringing Master Stephen into the world. A tragedy from which Sir Russell never fully recovered."

Noticing the light from tall windows to his right, Dr Alexander turned toward them and peered out. The lawns stretched as far as the eye could see and Dr Alexander realised just how isolated Russell Hall was. Upon hearing of Lady Russell's fate, the corners of Dr Alexander's mouth downturned and a strong melancholy descended upon his heart. Despite the grandeur of his surroundings, Dr Alexander could no longer perceive Sir Russell as the privileged gentleman he'd been. Instead, all he could fathom in his mind was the spectral image of a crooked, old man rattling about his even older home with little human contact and even less association with the outside world.

Dr Alexander shifted his gaze downward and, seeing Mr Snyder tending to his horse, felt his spirits lift. He was always impressed by the Bow Street Society horses' condition. Too many times, he'd come across malnourished, overworked horses on London's streets—many of whom were, tragically, beyond hope.

Sudden, deep sniffing from behind him pulled Dr Alexander from his musings, however. Turning toward it, he saw the slow moving form of a Staffordshire bull terrier tottering from a wicker basket at the foot of the bed. Dr Alexander smiled broadly and, crouching, offered his cupped hands to the dog. He said, "Come on, there's a good boy."

The dog stopped, sniffed the air, and continued to approach the stranger. Dr Alexander scrutinised how the animal moved—the way his paws distributed his weight, how his hips and elbows bent, and overall speed—as he came toward him. Though it wasn't blatant, Dr Alexander nonetheless spied a slight limp to the dog's gait and rigidness to his joints. He was also somewhat breathless by the time he reached him.

"There's a good boy, Claude," Dr Alexander said and ran a hand over the various parts of the bull terrier's head starting with the foreface at the front and moving upwards to the stop, backskull, and occiput. While resting one hand upon the dog's crest (the back of his neck), Dr Alexander slid his other across the dog's underjaw. Gently gripping the dog's snout next, Dr Alexander lifted Claude's lips to examine the gums and teeth. There was wear and yellowing of the teeth but nothing to be concerned about. Proceeding to examine the remainder of Claude, therefore, Dr Alexander slid his hands over the top of Claude's middle to examine his withers, back, loin, and croup.

After completing his inspection of these areas, Dr Alexander continued to Claude's point of shoulder and point of forechest at the front and the shoulder, ribcage, flank, brisket, and tuck. A quick check of the tail told Dr Alexander it was intact, while the dog's claws were as long as they ought to be. In personality, the bull terrier was both docile and friendly, sniffing and licking Dr Alexander's hands without growl or whimper. Encouraging the dog to turn toward the window, Dr Alexander lifted each eyelid and peered into Claude's eyes. "Cataracts," he remarked. Lifting Claude's front left forefoot—more commonly referred to as a paw by most— he held Claude's upper arm—aka, the top of his leg—at the same time and lifted the forefoot to bend Claude's elbow. The dog shifted his weight to his right forefoot and tried to step backward as Dr Alexander manipulated the joint. Dr Alexander could also feel some resistance against the movement coming from within the joint.

Lifting and dropping the left forefoot to check the rigidity of Claude's wrist, Dr Alexander's suspicions were confirmed as he felt resistance there, too. To be absolutely certain, however, he checked the rigidity of the joints at Claude's hips, points of hock—the angular part at the back of his rear legs—and ankles. When he manipulated each by lifting and bending Claude's legs, Dr Alexander felt the same resistance as before. Placing the hindfoot on the floor, Dr Alexander finally said, "And the onset of arthritis."

"Sir Russell purchased Claude when he was still a puppy," Mr Appleby said. Claude, having been given back his leg, sniffed the air and tottered over to the manservant. As with Dr Alexander, the dog showed no aggression toward Mr Appleby.

"How long ago was that?"

"About... eight... nine years ago?"

"Claude does seem a fair age," Dr Alexander remarked. The dog's brown fur was flecked with both white and grey. "Has he always slept in here?"

"For as far as I can remember," Mr Appleby replied.

"Can you describe to me what Sir Russell and Claude were likely to have done on the day Sir Russell died?"

"I can," Mr Appleby said, straightening, once he'd stroked behind the dog's ears. "I brought Sir Russell his breakfast at eight o'clock as usual. I'd put on some scraps from the previous night's dinner table for Claude. Sir Russell would read his morning newspaper for an hour and then I would assist him in dressing."

"Was it the case that day?"

"It was. After Sir Russell was dressed, he told me he would read for a while. His joints weren't what they were, either."

"So, you left him alone in here?"

"Yes. He must've decided to go downstairs, though, for, only an hour later, I heard a cry and then something heavy tumbling down the back stairs."

"The *back* stairs?"

"Yes. The Master felt more secure taking those because they were sturdier. We don't have as many servants as we once did, so it was unlikely Sir Russell would meet anyone on the way up or down, either. He enjoyed his privacy, you see."

"And you found him at the base of the stairs," Dr

Alexander thought aloud rather than enquired. Nonetheless, Mr Appleby nodded.

Taking a moment to survey the room, Dr Alexander next moved to the door, saying, "He finished reading and left the bedroom—does Claude always do that?"

"Do what?"

"Follow rather than heel?" Dr Alexander enquired, looking over his shoulder at the terrier standing approximately a foot away from him.

"I can't say I've noticed," Mr Appleby replied.

Dr Alexander pursed his lips together as he considered the matter a moment. Watching Claude over his shoulder still, he put one foot forward. The dog remained stationary, albeit sniffing the air. Taking another step forward, Dr Alexander continued to watch the animal's reaction. It chose to stay where it was until Dr Alexander walked at a proper pace, at which point, it followed but kept about a foot behind him at all times.

"Could you walk from the room, Mr Appleby?" Dr Alexander enquired as he returned to the middle of the bedroom with Claude still following. "I want to be certain Claude isn't keeping his distance because he's unsure of me."

Nodding, Mr Appleby gestured to the dog and called to him before leaving the room. Claude, having lifted his head at the sound of his name, sniffed the air, and followed the manservant in an identical fashion to Dr Alexander.

Dr Alexander smiled and enquired, "Now, will you go down the main stairs, please, Mr Appleby?"

"Yes, Doctor," the manservant replied. Leading Claude along the landing, with Dr Alexander following both at a fair distance, Mr Appleby paused at the stairs' summit and started to descend. Even with the hesitation, however, Claude had stopped and waited on the landing until Mr Appleby had reached the third step before following. Thus, the dog was nowhere near the man's feet or legs either at the start of his descent or at his end. Though Claude was near blind, he undoubtedly smelt where Mr Appleby was at any given point on the stairs, and thus kept his distance.

"Where are the back stairs? We must take Claude to them at once."

IV

Mr Treaves leant upon his cane as he observed Mr Heath's thorough inspection of the servants' stairs. Having used his tailor's measuring tape to identify the bottom step's height, Mr Heath had next measured its tread while squatting. His knees had soon come to rest upon the corridor's hard floor, however, as he'd exchanged the tape for a magnifying glass and scrutinised the tread's edge through it. He'd also run the flat of his hand across the entire length of the same edge before making circles across the wood. This same method was repeated for the next step up and the one after that. At present, he had one knee on the third and the other on the second while studying the first one and then the other through the magnifying glass. Fascinated by Mr Heath's methodology, Mr Treaves remained silent.

"How old are these stairs?" Mr Heath enquired as he jerked his hips back and forth to apply and release pressure upon the oak.

"As old as the house, I believe," Mr Treaves replied.

"Interesting," Mr Heath stated. After the third step was the first of two landings which not only served as resting points but also marked the changes in the flight's angles. From this first landing, another three steps ran off at a sharp ninety-degree angle to the second landing. Another ten steps ran off at another sharp ninety-degree angle from the second landing, this time mirroring the first set of steps in its direction.

"Did you know, Mr Treaves, most staircases don't exceed sixteen treads?" Mr Heath enquired as he straightened. Gesturing to the current structure, he added, "Even double quarter-landing stairs such as these. Mark," he lifted his finger, "three steps to the first landing, three steps to the second, and ten to the summit." He got to his feet and, climbing to the second landing, peered up at the summit. "These steps are very deep—undoubtedly to make the maximum use of this angular space, hence the choice of a double quarter-landing staircase rather than a single."

At that moment, the door at the summit opened and Dr Alexander came into view. Seeing his fellow Bow Streeter, he said, "Mr Heath, how fares your investigation?"

"It fares well enough, Doctor," he replied, climbing the remainder of the stairs toward the veterinarian. As he put his weight on the eighth step though, the oak creaked loudly beneath his foot. At once, he dropped to his knees and ran his hand over the wood, much to the astonishment of Mr Appleby behind Dr Alexander. Moving toward the summit, Mr Heath said, "Pardon me." Both Mr Appleby and Dr Alexander retreated and Mr Heath spent several minutes scrutinising the tenth step using his magnifying glass, the naked eye, and his sense of touch. Finally, he leapt to his feet and exclaimed, "I have it!" He pointed to the step, "The wood of this step is warped!"

"It is?" Mr Appleby enquired, bending over to take a closer look. "I don't see it."

"It *is* rather slight but it *is* there, I can assure you. The edge of the tread slants downward and mark," Mr Heath once more ran his hand over the wood, "the dip in the tread where many a foot has eroded the surface over the course of the staircase's lifetime."

"Oh yes, I feel it," Mr Appleby said after running his fingers over the indicated spot. Taking a firm grip of the doorway to steady himself as he straightened, he glanced down at Mr Treaves—whom was on the second landing, looking up at them—and enquired, "But what has this to do with Sir Russell's death?"

"It has *everything* to do with it," Mr Heath replied. Turning, he descended the stairs and joined the solicitor. Dr Alexander and Mr Appleby remained at the top, meanwhile. Mr Heath went on, "Mr Treaves has already told me Sir Russell felt unbalanced on the main stairs— which is why he had taken to using these. One can only assume, then, Sir Russell felt generally off-kilter. In which case, a misjudgement of his footing on the eroded section of tread could've easily sent him off-balance."

"So too could his catching his foot on his dog, however," Mr Treaves pointed out.

"Only in theory, not in practise," Dr Alexander replied. Half-turning toward the open doorway, he called to Claude and the terrier came tottering into view. Mr Appleby, to allow more space for the animal, moved away. Dr Alexander added, "Observe."

Facing Mr Heath and Mr Treaves once more, he began a slow descent of the stairs. Claude, having sniffed the air, neared the edge of the top step but waited until Dr Alexander had descended three of the steps before following. When Dr Alexander reached the second landing, and stopped, Claude halted where he was despite having his front paws lower than his back. Mr Heath and Mr Treaves pressed their backs against the wall as Dr Alexander continued his descent and the animal duly followed but kept a consistent distance.

"Mr Appleby and I tested Claude's behaviour on the main stairs, too," Dr Alexander explained, "but every time we descended—regardless of which of us it was—Claude kept a safe distance at all times. Therefore, Mr Treaves, I must insist this dog couldn't have possibly tripped his owner and caused his death."

"Could Claude have become excited by something and ran in front of Sir Russell though?" Mr Treaves suggested.

"No," Dr Alexander shook his head. "Aside from the fact Claude is as placid as a lake on a summer's day, his joints are showing the first symptoms of arthritis. Thus, even if he had become excited, he could not have moved quickly enough to catch up to Sir Russell, pass him, and get under his feet on the stairs. Additionally, Claude has cataracts. He wouldn't have been able to see a cat, or a mouse, or the like, even if it was standing in front of him. Certainly, he could've picked up its scent but, in my professional experience, I think it more likely a dog of Claude's years would've barked rather than run at an intruder to his territory. Even this, I find unlikely in Claude's case, however, for he hasn't showed any aggression toward me despite having been introduced to me only today."

"It is conclusive, then," Mr Treaves said with a broad smile. "Claude is innocent of any wrong doing and the stairs, coupled with Sir Russell's advanced years, were solely responsible for his accident."

"Without question," Mr Heath replied.

"That is *tremendous* news, Dr Alexander, Mr Heath. I can now, finally, carry out the last wishes of my dear, departed friend. Thank you, sirs. Thank you from the bottom of mine—and Claude's—heart." The solicitor clasped each of the Bow Streeter's hands in turn and shook them vigorously. Claude, who'd been once more sniffing the air, gave a loud yawn and lay down on the landing. Soon, the sound of snoring could be heard coming from the animal, and all four men chuckled with hearty amusement.

The Case of the Eerie Encounter

I

HORROR AT
BAKER STREET STATION

The wondrous marvel of the underground railway paid witness to a scene of utter horror last eve when a man purportedly fell beneath a train.

Mister Frank Denman, as he has now been identified, was seen falling onto the tracks by his fellow travellers at four p.m. yesterday. Seconds later, the train arriving at Baker Street station passed over him, despite the driver's valiant efforts to avoid catastrophe.

By fate's hand, Doctor Percival Weeks— whose long-standing association with the Metropolitan Police at Scotland Yard has been well documented by this newspaper— was present. Tragically, the medical assistance administered by Doctor Weeks in the immediate aftermath was unable to stem the poor man's blood flow. Mister Denman passed away shortly thereafter.

"He had drunk whiskey at the bar," a witness—who preferred to remain nameless here—told your correspondent. The spoken 'he' being a reference to Mister Denman. "Then he stood," my witness continued, "Walked to the platform's edge, waited 'til the train come, and just *went!*" A gentleman, who'd overheard my witness' exclamation, offered his own conjecture upon the matter.

He said, "He jumped. There's nothing for a man to trip on, and no one was near him."

Rapid knocking stirred Miss Trent from her reading. Discarding Tuesday morning's edition of the *Gaslight Gazette,* she went to investigate. As she passed, the hall's grandfather clock chimed eight thirty—an early caller indeed! With this in mind, she slid back the heavy bolts, turned a key, and opened the Bow Street Society's front door.

"Good morning, Miss Trent," a narrow-faced woman stated the moment her dark-brown eyes met Miss Trent's hazel. A dry, coarse hand extended toward Miss Trent, holding a calling card. "I'm Mrs Madeleine Snelling. I hope you shall forgive my unexpected visit when you hear what I have to say." A short pause followed. "May I come in?"

"Of course." Miss Trent stepped aside. Having taken, and read, the card while Mrs Snelling introduced herself, Miss Trent slipped it into her pocket. Ending at her waist, the thick jacket matched Miss Trent's burgundy bustle skirts in colour. Beneath these, she wore dense, woollen, black stockings. Her tight corset, beneath the dual layers of jacket and blouse, provided additional protection against the chilled air. It also served to enhance the natural, inward curve of her waist. Chestnut-brown, corkscrew ringlets lay between her shoulders, while her remaining hair was curled, and pinned, into a tight bun upon her crown.

Closing the front door and sliding its bolts back into place, she led her visitor to the parlour. Mrs Snelling halted the moment she entered the room, however. Staring at the newspaper lying upon the overstuffed, tête-à-tête sofa, she enquired, 'You have read of yesterday's ghastly event at Baker Street station?"

"Yes," Miss Trent replied. Stepping around her, she took the newspaper from the sofa and placed it behind the clock on the mantel piece.

The sofa's high back had a triple balloon shape to it, while its navy-blue fabric matched an armchair facing the door. The sofa looked to the hearth on the parlour's left side. Both pieces had heavy, worsted fringes, bullions hanging from their arms, and embroidered light-blue leaves.

A low, oak table with curved legs and feet resembling paws—known as Queen Anne feet—stood before the sofa. It was placed upon a rug whose colour, fringing, and embroidered design matched those of the seating. In the back, right corner of the parlour, a bookcase stood against the light blue and bronze gilt wallpaper.

The previously mentioned fireplace had an oak surround featuring hand-carved floral embellishments down each side and a flat mantel shelf on top. Lumps of coal, orange with heat, sat in a pile within its iron hearth. An oil painting, depicting a bleak and wild Hampstead Heath, hung upon the chimney breast.

Once she and Mrs Snelling had settled upon the sofa and armchair respectively, Miss Trent enquired, "Did you know Mr Denman?"

"*No*," Mrs Snelling snapped, though her tone was more firm than angry. Due to her lips barely moving, her voice had also sounded nasal. Sitting erect upon the armchair's edge, her hands clasped in her lap and her gaze fixed upon Miss Trent, she continued. "My *son*, Jerome—who has been but eighteen years on this earth—is insistent he has met Mr Denman, however."

"Which you consider to be ill fortune…?" Miss Trent hazarded.

"I *do*. My son has—" Mrs Snelling cut herself off and pursed her lips. After a moment, she said, "…He has no work to speak of—though it's not for want of trying." With a satisfied expression, she glanced at her hands and gave a curt nod. "Yesterday, when poor Mr Denman was breathing his last at Baker Street station, my son claims to have spoken with him."

"I don't understand—"

"I'm being unclear," Mrs Snelling interrupted. "I don't mean to be, I assure you. The whole thing is simply *preposterous*!"

"Please, take your time," Miss Trent smiled. "I have plenty of it."

"Thank you, Miss Trent," Mrs Snelling's taut lips morphed into a smile. A swift recollection of her surroundings dispersed it, however. "My son was at home at four o'clock yesterday afternoon. This morning, upon reading of Mr Denman's ghastly accident in the newspaper, my son told me he had spoken to him at four o'clock precisely. Jerome said he'd introduced himself as Mister Frank Denman and stated he was looking for a friend—Mister Archibald. Naturally, my son informed him no one of that name dwelt at our address. Mr Denman had next enquired how long we'd resided in the house. My son informed him of the answer—three years. Mr Denman then obtained directions to Baker Street station and left."

"How could your son be so certain it was the same Mister Denman?"

"He cannot, but, nonetheless, he *insists* it to be the one and the same man. *Please*, Miss Trent. I'm worried about Jerome. Could the Society convince him of his foolishness?"

Miss Trent couldn't help but frown at the prospect of convincing an eighteen-year-old boy of anything. Yet, she was, admittedly, intrigued by the story. It also fulfilled the Society's criteria for case acceptance. She therefore smiled and replied, "Of course, Mrs Snelling. I'll arrange for two of our members to visit upon you and your son this afternoon. If you would be so kind as to give me your address?"

Mrs Snelling's body became rigid and she stared at Miss Trent a moment. "Yes," she said, with a rapid blinking of her eyes and slight shake of her head. "I'll write it down for you…" Her voice trailed off as she rummaged in her pockets. Miss Trent, having stood from the sofa and gone to the bookshelf, returned with both pencil and paper in hand. "Oh, thank you," Mrs Snelling mumbled upon taking them. Hastily writing down her address, she offered the items back to Miss Trent. "Whom should I expect?"

II

"Mr Maxwell, a pleasure to make your acquaintance once more," Mr Gregory Elliott commented in his usual monotone. In his late twenties, Mr Elliott could be described as beautiful rather than handsome. Fair—almost translucent—skin graced his slender face. Undefined cheekbones were crowned by unflinching, green-brown eyes, while his nose was narrow from bridge to tip. Short, very dark brown—almost black—hair was combed and well maintained. His attire consisted of a midnight-blue frockcoat, cravat, and waistcoat. The last of which had a silver design embroidered into its front panels. Hanging across one side of his waistcoat was the silver chain of a pocket watch, while a silver pin was affixed to his cravat. In addition to all this, he wore a plain, white, high-collared shirt and some black trousers. Peering down his nose at his Bow Street Society colleague—Mr Elliott being several inches taller than Mr Maxwell—he extended his hand and added, "Also, congratulations on your appointment to journalist."

"Thank you, Mr Elliott," Mr Joseph Maxwell replied, wiping his palm upon his black frockcoat before shaking the offered hand. Younger than Mr Elliott—twenty-one years to Mr Elliott's twenty-eight, to be precise—Mr Maxwell was equally clean shaven. Beneath his green eyes, freckles covered his high cheekbones. Dark-auburn hair, parted on the left, matched his eyelashes and brows in colour. Maxwell was also fair skinned, though not as pale or as translucent as Mr Elliott.

"Would you care to do the honours?" Mr Elliott enquired, gesturing toward the Snelling's front door. Their street comprised of terraced houses with neat gardens, large bay windows, and swept front steps. The quality of the houses' brick and paintwork denoted their occupants' middle class status but, overall, the street held a peaceful, pleasant atmosphere.

"Oh! Y—yes, of course!" Mr Maxwell exclaimed,

feeling his cheeks warm. Taking a moment to straighten his cravat and frockcoat, he swung open the gate and strode up the path to the front door. There, he cleared his throat—louder than was necessary—and rapped his knuckles against the stained-glass window.

At once, the curtain in the window to their right was pulled back and a boy's blood-drained face peered out. His hazel eyes darted between the men, while his bony fingers kept a tight grip upon the curtain. The boy's thin knees were smothered by a patchwork quilt tucked around his waist. He sat upon a high-backed dining chair at an angle to the window. Though the window's lock was within the boy's reach, he didn't relinquish his grip upon the curtain until a heartbeat before Mr Maxwell and Mr Elliott heard the front door's bolt.

"Good afternoon, gentlemen. May I help you?" Mrs Snelling enquired through thin lips.

"Mr Gregory Elliott and Mr Joseph Maxwell from the Bow Street Society, madam. To whom are we speaking?"

"Your client, Mr Elliott," Mrs Snelling stated, drily. Stepping aside, she added, "I'm Mrs Snelling. Please—" Violent gasps from within the house cut her off, however. Abandoning the two men on the step, she rushed through a door on the right and allowed it to swing ajar. Mr Elliott and Mr Maxwell, who'd remained outside, exchanged glances. The latter then went to cross the threshold.

"Wait," Mr Elliott hissed, grasping Mr Maxwell's arm.

"She was about to invite us in," Mr Maxwell pointed out.

The sound of the sash window being thrown up at once distracted them though. Stepping backward, the two Bow Streeters were met by the sight of Mrs Snelling shoving the boy's head outside. The latter took rapid, shallow breaths between harsh coughs, while his lean fingers gripped his chest and throat, his body trembled, and sweat formed upon his brow.

"Deep breaths, Jerome," Mrs Snelling advised, her voice lacking its earlier strictness. While her arm wrapped around his emaciated form, she retrieved a cup of strong, black coffee from a hidden table. As he took a sip from it, though, another coughing fit took him and he projected the hot, dark liquid through the open window, toward Mr Elliott and Mr Maxwell. The two men darted backward, causing Mr Maxwell to stumble against the boundary wall as he did so. Mrs Snelling meanwhile pulled her son back inside, and shut the window.

"We should help," Mr Maxwell remarked, again trying to enter the house but, again, being drawn back by Mr Elliott.

"We're not doctors."

"Then why are *we* here and not Doctor Locke or—or Doctor Weeks?" Mr Maxwell questioned, as he freed his arm and straightened his frock coat's lapels and skirt several times.

"The utilisation of conjecture and surmising is ill advised when one's work is identifying fact, Mr Maxwell. A statement, I suspect, you would agree with given your profession."

"I would," Maxwell nodded. "But we shan't find any facts standing out here."

"A thousand pardons, gentlemen," Mrs Snelling said as she emerged from the house, causing Mr Maxwell to jump. Her voice was soft as she wrung her hands. "You weren't meant to see such a sight."

"Your son is gravely ill," Mr Elliott observed.

"I was going to come inside, but—" Mr Maxwell began, looking to his colleague, but being interrupted by Mrs Snelling.

"Oh *no*," she shook her head. "No, no. Jerome's turns worsen when in the company of strangers."

"And yet he spoke to Mr Denman," Mr Elliott remarked.

"Through the window," Mrs Snelling pointed to it. "He is much better inside, usually. He must've seen you."

"He did. We are going to have to speak with him in person, however, if we are to honour the Society's commitment," Mr Elliott replied.

Mrs Snelling glanced over her shoulder as she wrung her hands more. Finally, she gave a small nod. "You'd better come inside, then," she replied and led them into the hallway. Once they'd regrouped, she added, "Wait here a moment." For a second time, she disappeared into the other room, this time closing its door completely.

Mr Maxwell glanced around the dim, sparsely furnished hallway. His index finger tapped upon the skirt of his frock coat while Mrs Snelling and Jerome's hushed, muffled voices drifted through the wood. Every now and then, his nose caught the waft of burning paper. Shifting his weight from one foot to the other, Mr Maxwell looked to Mr Elliott with a weak smile.

"What are you *doing*?" he whispered, his eyes wide, when he saw Mr Elliott sifting through a pile of opened envelopes on a table by the front door. Maxwell shot a worried glance toward Mrs Snelling's room but nonetheless joined his colleague. Mr Elliott, who hadn't acknowledged Mr Maxwell's question, held a typed letter. The few words Maxwell could read in those brief moments were *appointment, your son,* and *Monday.*

Mrs Snelling's reappearance compelled him to turn upon his heels, however, in an attempt to shield Mr Elliott. Certain they'd been caught, Maxwell stood bolt upright as he felt his chest tighten, his heart race, and sweat form upon his temples and palms.

"Has he agreed to see us?" Mr Elliott enquired, stepping out from behind him.

"He has, but he wants me to stay with him," Mrs Snelling replied.

"I have no argument against such an arrangement," Mr Elliott said. Looking to Mr Maxwell, he enquired, "Do you, Mr Maxwell?"

"*No,*" Mr Maxwell replied in a high-pitched voice. Both Mr Elliott and Mrs Snelling stared at him in equal confusion, though the former's emotion failed to register upon his features. Clearing his throat under the others' scrutiny, Mr Maxwell added, "No, of course not." He cleared his throat once more, "Lead on, Mrs Snelling."

When they entered the small parlour, the scent of burning paper strengthened as the two men caught sight of its source. The boy—again sitting by the window—held a china saucer upon the arm of his chair. Laid upon the saucer were pieces of brown paper being steadily burnt to create wisps of smoke which the boy inhaled. Though not a doctor, Mr Elliott had listened to medical practitioners giving testimony about such a treatment during the course of criminal case proceedings. Prior to burning, the paper would've been dipped in a strong solution of salt-petre— also known as salt-peter or nitrate of potash—and dried. Today, this same chemical is more commonly referred to as potassium nitrate and is used as a food preservative. It's toxic in high doses, both today and in 1896, however. From Mr Elliott's observation of the boy, he could see no ill effect from the smoke. Nevertheless, he chose to sit at the opposite end of the sofa to the boy when invited to do so by Mrs Snelling. Mr Maxwell, who'd coughed when nearing Mrs Snelling's son, had also retreated and taken the spot beside his colleague.

"Jerome, this is Misters Elliott and Maxwell from the Bow Street Society," Mrs Snelling informed the boy. At his meek nod, she looked to the two men and added, "Gentlemen, this is my son, Jerome."

"Hello," Mr Maxwell replied with a lift of his hand.

"Why did you not inform Miss Trent of your son's asthma?" Mr Elliott enquired once Jerome had passed the saucer to his mother, and its contents were extinguished within the hearth. "She would have assigned a doctor to your case, rather than a journalist and a criminal defence solicitor."

"You are a journalist?" Mrs Snelling enquired, wide eyed.

"No, I'm the solicitor," Mr Elliott replied. "Mr Maxwell is a journalist with the *Gaslight Gazette*. You may rely on his discretion as much as mine, however."

"Absolutely," Maxwell agreed, stifling another cough.

"We don't require a doctor," Mrs Snelling stated, her tone strict once more. Standing at Jerome's side, she remarked, "My son has seen plenty of those." Mr Maxwell glanced at Mr Elliott, recalling the letter he had found in the hallway, but Mr Elliott's gaze remained on Mrs Snelling, who added, "We need you to clear up the matter regarding Mister Denman."

"I *know* what I saw," Jerome interjected. Everyone at once looked to him with a variety of reactions—his mother with concern, Mr Elliott with stoicism, and Mr Maxwell with surprise at the boy's assertive tone and manner. Devoid of any breathing troubles, Jerome continued, "He was standing on the other side of *this* window. I shall swear it upon the Bible if I must."

"Mr Snelling," Mr Elliott began, leaning forward.

Jerome at once retreated within his chair and grasped his mother's hand. His lips also trembled as Mr Maxwell noticed a bead of sweat forming upon the boy's brow. Movement in the corner of Mr Maxwell's eyes also drew him to the fingers of Jerome's other hand. They were twisting the quilt's edge and holding it with such strength, his knuckles whitened.

In the meantime, Mr Elliott continued, "Both Mr Maxwell and I seek out the truth on a daily basis during the course of our respective professions. This is all we seek today. We are interested in neither humiliating you nor discrediting you. If you refuse to speak with us though, I shall guarantee we will return tomorrow, and the next day, and the day after, until you do. Your mother has hired the Bow Street Society, and it—and we—are obliged to honour the commitment made."

Jerome remained silent for a time. His hands retained their grip upon Mrs Snelling's hand and the quilt, however. Finally, he nodded. "Very well," he said, to his mother's obvious relief. "What do you want to know?"

"What time did you see Mr Denman yesterday?" Mr Elliott enquired.

"Four o'clock," Jerome replied.

"How can you be so certain?"

"I checked my pocket watch."

"May we see it?"

Mrs Snelling tightened her grip upon her son's hand and Jerome glanced up at her. She looked to Mr Elliott and Mr Maxwell though. Her face had also become a little pale and, for a time, Jerome looked between her and their guests with a frown that deepened the longer she remained silent. "Show them your watch, Jerome," Mrs Snelling eventually stated in a flat, low-key voice. "There's a good boy."

"Y—yes, Mother," Jerome replied, his own voice heavy with concern. Fumbling around in his tunic's pocket, he brought out a gold pocket watch. "It was my father's," he explained as he pulled his hand from his mother's and flipped open the watch's cover. Mr Elliott had observed Mrs Snelling's fingers tighten before she'd relinquished Jerome's hand. Rather than remark upon it though, he instead made a note of it in his mind, and retrieved his own pocket watch. Opening it, he held it beside Jerome's and compared the time between the two faces—they matched. A quick glance around the room also confirmed to Mr Elliott the watch had been Jerome's only means of checking the time.

"Thank you," Mr Elliott said, putting his own watch away. As Jerome did the same, Mr Elliott enquired, "Do you wind the watch yourself?"

"I do it for him," Mrs Snelling interjected.

"I'm not entirely sure how to myself," Jerome added.

"Mr Denman asked you for directions to Baker Street station, didn't he?" Mr Maxwell enquired. At Jerome's nod, Mr Maxwell probed, "Did he say *why* he was going there?"

"No," Jerome replied.

"Mr Snelling, may you please explain how you are so certain it was *the* Mister Denman you saw at the window?" Mr Elliott enquired.

"He told me his name. I saw no deceit in him so believe it to be so."

"Perhaps, if it were to be arranged, you could visit the morgue to look upon the dead man's face and confirm if he is, indeed, the one you saw at the window—"

"*No!*" Jerome cried, leaping to his feet. With contorted features, wide eyes, and trembling body, his gaze darted between them in the same manner as before. "I *shan't* do it! I *shan't*!" He'd twisted his body toward his mother, to Mr Elliott and Mr Maxwell, and back again whilst he'd yelled. All of a sudden, he threw himself back down into his chair and gripped his chest. Unlike previously though, he did not gasp or wheeze but, instead, swayed and trembled.

"I must ask you to *leave*, gentlemen," Mrs Snelling commanded. "You'll forgive me, I hope, for not showing you to the door."

"Of course," Mr Elliott replied.

"Th—thank you for your time," Mr Maxwell said, and followed his colleague from the house. Only once he'd heard the front door close behind them did he release his held breath.

"A peculiar child," Mr Elliott remarked, leading the way through the gate.

"Very," Mr Maxwell agreed, falling into step beside him. "I can tell you now, Mr Elliott, he does *not* have asthma." At Mr Elliott's questioning gaze, Mr Maxwell prodded his own chest with his thumb and explained, "*I* have suffered enough from my nerves to recognise the same in another."

"More conjecture, Mr Maxwell?" Mr Elliott enquired with an uncharacteristic frown.

"Yes, but conjecture grounded in experience."

"The doctor who wrote to Mrs Snelling does have a reputation for treating ailments of the mind, in addition to afflictions of the body. Nonetheless, I think it would be prudent of us to reserve judgement until we are in possession of all the facts. Come, let us travel to Baker Street station."

III

Opened on the tenth of January 1863, Baker Street station was one of five along a railway line between Paddington, Bishop's Road, and Farringdon Street. The others being Edgware Road, Portland Road, Gower Street, and King's Cross. The entire line was owned, and constructed, by the Metropolitan Railway Company. It was that company's engineer in chief, Sir John Fowler, who oversaw the line's original construction.

When it was first built, Baker Street station consisted of a pair of single storey buildings on the north and south corners of Marylebone Road and Baker Street. Within these buildings was the booking office, where passengers could purchase tickets, and stairs down to the west end of the platforms. By 1896, six further platforms— all above ground—had been built on the Baker Street station's north side. The initial two served as an extension to Swiss Cottage, while the additional four linked to the existing line. They also made the north westwards extension of the line possible. This extension took the line into Middlesex, Buckinghamshire, and Hertfordshire. Eventually, in 1892, this same extension had reached Aylesbury and Verney Junction.

It was via the stairs at Baker Street's south corner that Mr Elliott and Mr Maxwell gained access to the platform where Mr Denman had died. A brief conversation with the booking office's ticket master had yielded the name of the guard who'd been on duty. The two Bow Streeters were also informed of this same guard being on duty again today. Mr Maxwell paused at the foot of the stairs to allow his eyes to adjust to the gloom. Though there were large, globe gaslights hanging from the brick-barrelled, vaulted ceiling, the sulphurous smoke of the train's steam engine—and sheer volume of people—made seeing one's way difficult. Even the inclusion of skylights—constructed using thick glass on the surface to capture natural daylight, and lined with white tiles to maximum the light carried to the platform—were not sufficient to dispel the perpetual dusk over the area. Indeed, the huge, oval eyelet holes—also lined with tiles and intended to provide both air and light to the travellers below—did little to ease the overwhelming sense of suffocation one felt when standing upon the platform.

Mr Elliott, who'd walked ahead of Mr Maxwell, took refuge against the platform's curved wall. With every inch covered by a disordered collage of advertisements—selling everything from sunlight soap to theatre tickets—the wall provided less of a sanctuary from chaos than the platform itself. Nonetheless, there he stood, his handkerchief pressed over his mouth and nose, as the train eased forward and departed the station with a billowing of smoke and a shriek of its whistle.

"Ah, there you are," Mr Maxwell remarked upon finally locating Mr Elliott. Noticing the handkerchief, Mr Maxwell frowned and inwardly scolded himself for not having thought of the precaution.

"And *there* is our guard," Mr Elliott replied, walking past his colleague to a short man in a dark uniform standing at the platform's edge. A whistle dropped from the man's mouth and, by a chain hung about his neck, rested against his broad chest.

"Yessir?" the man greeted as they approached.

"Are you Mr Kemp, the guard who was on duty yesterday?" Mr Elliott enquired.

"Yessir," Mr Kemp confirmed with a firm nod.

"Excellent. I'm Mr Gregory Elliott and this is my associate, Mr Joseph Maxwell, We are members of the Bow Street Society—"

"Bow Street *Society*, y'say?" Mr Kemp replied with barefaced awe.

"*Yes*," Mr Elliott stated. "We wish to speak to you about Mr Denman—"

"*Terrible* business, sir, *terrible* business. The Lor' have mercy upon his soul."

"You subscribe to the theory he committed

suicide, then?"

"That I do, sir. That I do."

"What time did he fall—I mean, jump?" Mr Maxwell interjected, wiping his forehead with his handkerchief. The air was heavy and hot, despite the cold winds and freezing rain on the streets above.

"Four o'clock on the dot, sir," Mr Kemp replied. Taking his shining pocket watch from his tunic, he tapped its case and added, "I keep a close eye on the train's comin's and goin's."

"You couldn't have been mistaken?" Mr Maxwell challenged, glancing at his—now sooty—handkerchief.

"No, sir! I checked the time as soon as I saw the train's lamplight in the tunnel. Straight after, I heard a shriek—not the train's whistle, mind you, but a woman's—and I went running to where Mr Denman lay on the tracks. I lifted my whistle but… the train had no hopes of stopping, sirs. Poor old Finnegan sent down the brakes—Lor', there was a lot of sparks!—but the engine's too 'eavy. It went over Denman as clean as you like."

"Who identified the body?" Mr Maxwell enquired.

"I don't know, sir. The coppers sorted all that out."

"Thank you, Mr Kemp," Mr Elliott said with a firm shake of the guard's hand. "You've been most helpful."

IV

The Snellings' parlour fire burned brightly within the hearth while rain thrashed the sash window. Mrs Snelling had lit a lamp against the encroaching gloom while Jerome had remained in his chair, watching Mr Elliott and Mr Maxwell as they sat across from him on the sofa.

"I'd thought our business done," Jerome remarked, his fingers once again twisting a patch of the quilt covering his knees.

"And soon it shall be," Mr Elliott replied. "Your mother hired the Bow Street Society because she was concerned about you. You were insisting you had seen Mr Denman at precisely the time when he was, reportedly, dying on the tracks of Baker Street station. After speaking with Mr Kemp—the guard on duty at Baker Street when Mr Denman breathed his last—I may now tell you both," Mr Elliott glanced at Mrs Snelling, "You are both correct."

"I don't understand," Jerome said, looking from Mr Elliott, to Mr Maxwell, to his mother, and back at the first.

"At some point during the course of yesterday, your pocket watch gained an hour. I can't be clearer with the details—I'm not a clockmaker—but pocket watch mechanisms are very delicate things. If yours became stuck, or increased in its speed for whatever reason, it could have caused this inconsistency in time keeping. In short, Mr Snelling, you spoke with Mr Denman at *three* o'clock and *not* four o'clock, as your watch told it to be."

"So you believe I *did* speak with him?" Jerome enquired, the corners of his mouth lifting a little.

"Without a doubt," Mr Maxwell interjected.

"And my watch was at fault," Jerome said as a full smile brightened his pale face.

"Precisely," Mr Elliott confirmed. Rising to his feet, he added, "I would recommend taking it to a clockmaker. Mrs Snelling, I have the name of one such tradesman who comes highly recommended. If you'd care to join Mr Maxwell and me in the hallway, I shall give it to you."

"Of course," Mrs Snelling replied. Giving Jerome's shoulder a gentle squeeze, she kissed the top of his head and followed Mr Elliott and Mr Maxwell into the hallway. Closing the door behind her, she turned toward them with a smile—only to have it vanish when she saw their sombre expressions.

"It is my *actual* recommendation, Mrs Snelling, you open your heart to your son and confess the truth of this matter to him," Mr Elliott told her, his natural monotone made all the colder by the anger in his eyes.

"I… I don't understand—"

"You were the one who put Jerome's watch forward," Mr Maxwell said.

"*Why* would I do that?" Mrs Snelling demanded, looking between them. Despite her words though, her voice lacked any hint of the indignation one would expect to hear from someone wrongfully accused.

"For a long time now, you've thought your son suffered with asthma," Mr Maxwell began. "When, in fact, he suffers from a highly sensitive, nervous disposition. I recognised it because—I'm sorry to say—I, too, am the same." He cleared his throat.

"I think you have only recently begun to suspect the truth, however," Mr Elliott said. "Hence your continued use of the smoke of burning brown paper soaked in nitrate of potash, to treat his condition. Nonetheless, your suspicions were strong enough to compel you to seek advice from Doctor Carnes. By happenstance, I noticed he was the signatory of a letter you'd left on your hall table. A name alone wouldn't be sufficient to inform me of your intentions with regards to your son—not under normal circumstances, anyway. Even the contents of the letter were too vague to pinpoint the nature of the appointment you'd had with him on Monday. No, I knew you wanted to speak to him about your son's nerves because I've encountered Doctor Carnes many times before during the course of criminal case proceedings. More often than not, Doctor Carnes gave witness testimony in support of a defendant's plea of not guilty by reason of insanity."

"Like most women responsible for running a household, you'll have a daily routine which you religiously adhere to," Mr Maxwell said. "Jerome would know of this routine." Mr Maxwell frowned, "You love your son, Mrs Snelling. The way you comforted him when he was having a turn proved that. You want to protect him, which is why, I think, you didn't want him to know about your appointment with Doctor Carnes. You couldn't go to the appointment without disrupting your routine, though. If you disrupted your routine, then Jerome would ask questions. So, to avoid that, you set his watch forward an hour. You probably left it that way for a few days before your appointment. The day after the appointment—today, in fact—you set the watch back to the correct time. All was well… until Jerome read the story about Mr Denman's death in the newspaper."

"You'd already arranged for Doctor Carnes to visit upon your son—possibly in the next few days—correct?" Mr Elliott enquired.

"Yes…" Mrs Snelling replied with a subdued tone and nod of her head. "…Friday, at one."

"He already knew of your son's nerves. If he should hear your son claiming he'd seen a dead man at the time of that man's death, you feared Doctor Carnes would insist on committing him. For all you want help for your son, you don't want *that* fate for him," Mr Elliott said.

Again, Mrs Snelling nodded but she didn't speak. Instead, she kept her head bowed and her gaze fixed to the floor.

Mr Elliott continued, "You had to convince Jerome of his mistake, before Doctor Carnes' visit, but he wouldn't listen to you. That's when you approached the Bow Street Society."

"Yes… it's true… all of it," Mrs Snelling lifted her head to show her eyes, glistening with unshed tears. "I did it for *him.* With his father gone, Jerome is *all* I have."

"I don't like being a party to *deception*, Mrs Snelling," Mr Elliott snapped. "I'll be recommending to Miss Trent she take no monies for your commission. If I'd known the true nature of it, I wouldn't have agreed to investigate. It conflicts with my—usually high—moral standards. I may be a defence solicitor but I nonetheless believe in the sanctity of fact, honesty, and decency. While there is no doubt your actions were borne from good intentions and a noble heart, you still endeavoured to make us," Mr Elliott glanced at Mr Maxwell, "and the Bow Street Society accessories *after* the fact. So, as I said before, open your heart to your son and confess your crime. He shall know, as we do, your motives were well founded—if poorly executed."

"I shall," Mrs Snelling replied. Swallowing hard, she took a moment to compose herself and continued, "And I deeply regret deceiving you both as I did—Miss Trent, too. Please know, though, how much I am grateful to you both for giving me the chance to tell Jerome myself— and for convincing him of his error."

"We said we'd honour our commitment to you, Mrs Snelling," Mr Maxwell reminded her. "And we have."

"All we ask, is you do us the same courtesy by making amends with your son," Mr Elliott added. At Mrs Snelling's final reassurances she would, indeed, do as they'd requested, Mr Elliott turned and left the house. Mr Maxwell followed behind but neither spoke as they walked down the path and embarked upon their respective journeys home.

The Case of the Christmas Crisis

I

The year was almost over. Summer was a distant memory, and winter had moved in. Rain had been a frequent visitor during the first half of December but, as the holy day of Christmas approached, snow showers took its place. In the early hours of the seventeenth, an earthquake shock had brought excitement to many across England and Wales— particularly those in the western counties.

Yet, as more snow descended upon Bow Street, thoughts of this occurrence were far from Miss Georgina Dexter's mind. Sitting at a dilapidated table within the kitchen of the Bow Street Society's house, she hummed *O, Holy Night* while threading twine through a packing needle's eye. Working in the light of a kerosene lamp, she sifted through laurel, ivy, and mistletoe until she found a fresh, curled holly leaf. This she speared with the packing needle's point before pushing the needle through and guiding the leaf along the twine to its knotted end. After adjusting the leaf's orientation, she delved into the mass of greenery to repeat the process.

The tip of Miss Dexter's petite nose was red despite the stove's warmth at her back. Her usually light tone was also deeper and, every now and then, she'd sniff and give a small cough. Nonetheless her fair skin remained pink in its complexion, while her green eyes paid careful attention to her slender hands' work. Yellow lamplight danced over her forest-green blouse and auburn hair. The former covered her entire bosom and matched her bustle skirts in colour, while the latter was wrapped into a large bun against the back of her neck. Tiny balls of light appeared and disappeared as the plain, silver hair pins and brooch she wore caught the lamplight when she moved. Though aged eighteen, Miss Dexter's diminutive stature and proportions gave her the appearance of someone much younger.

"That bough's up," Mr Samuel Snyder's rough, east end of London-accented voice remarked from the doorway. Brown, beady eyes, warmed by the lifting of his rotund cheeks by his smile, met Miss Dexter's when she looked up. His larger-than-average hand was lifted with its thumb pointed over his shoulder. Unlike Miss Dexter, Mr Snyder was broad in build—and taller, too. His own nose was perpetually reddened, while his complexion was coarse and dry. Even the thumb he held aloft was calloused and cracked. The sleeves of his off-white shirt were rolled up to his elbows, sweat droplets had formed in his black, bushy sideburns, and his short hair was more unkempt than usual. Patches of dust spotted his dark brown trousers and worn, black leather boots.

"I surrender," Miss Rebecca Trent declared from the table's other end. Putting the torn piece of brown paper she'd been attempting to sew leaves onto down, she said, "I'm too heavy handed for this."

"I'm happy to finish it, if you'd like?" Miss Dexter replied with a smile.

"Would you?" Miss Trent enquired. At Miss Dexter's nod, Miss Trent at once smiled and sighed. "*Thank* you." She put the materials before Miss Dexter and, standing, wiped her hands upon her apron. To Mr Snyder, she enquired, "You put the bough around the handrail?"

"Yeah," he replied. Taking a seat opposite Miss Dexter, he watched Miss Trent prepare some tea at the stove.

In her late twenties, Miss Trent was younger than Mr Snyder's forty-odd years. Attired in a burgundy jacket with matching bustle skirts, her clothes were far more ornamental compared to Miss Dexter's. The jacket's lapels were silk, and framed a stark-white blouse with three vertical lines of ruffles down its centre and a gold and ivory brooch pinned to its high neck. A broad, black belt with brass buckle separated her jacket and skirts. The latter having a light burgundy, front, lace panel. The tight curls of her chestnut-brown hair were pinned atop her head with a few loose strands permitted to hang down her back.

Dark-brown eyes looked to the snow-streaked window and bleak, afternoon sky beyond as she remarked, "I suppose it doesn't matter how long it takes us to decorate the house, as long as it's done by Christmas Day." Pouring steaming water into a teapot, she added the last onto a tray with three cups and saucers, a jug of cream, and a sugar bowl.

"How shall you make merry on Christmas Day, Miss Trent?" Miss Dexter enquired as the Bow Street Society clerk joined them at the table.

"My aunt has written, inviting me to stay with her in Tonbridge," Miss Trent replied. "Which would be lovely… for a day." She gave a weak smile. "I'm too accustomed to the unpredictable liveliness of London."

"Family's still family, though," Mr Snyder pointed out. "Some folks've got none."

"Still, you're welcome to share Christmas Day with us, Miss Trent," Miss Dexter added.

"Thank you, Miss Dexter," Miss Trent replied with a warmer smile. Setting the table with the tea things, she next picked up the pot and gave its contents a stir. Replacing it to stew awhile, she remarked, "Christmas has snuck up on me this year, it seems."

"Time's flown," Mr Snyder said. Folding his large arms across his chest, he continued, "The London to Brighton run woz back in November but it feels like it woz only yesterday." He smirked, "The weather woz more dreary, then."

"I can imagine it being rather exciting," Miss Dexter remarked, her features lifted by her wide smile. Guiding another holly leaf along the twine, she laid her creation upon the table and, while holding it, leant forward with wistfulness in her eyes. "Seeing the horseless carriages and…what were the others, Sam?"

"They called 'em 'motor cars'," Mr Snyder replied. "And it *woz* excitin', but *very* wet. Most drivers didn't have roofs," Mr Snyder chuckled. "No wonder only some got to Brighton. Still…" He gave a nod. "The start of the run woz sumin' to see. There's even talk of 'em doin' it again next year—"

The sudden sound of hurried knocking interrupted Mr Snyder, however. Though he and Miss Dexter looked toward the hallway, Miss Trent went to investigate. "The tea should be ready to pour now," she remarked before she left the room.

Further knocking filled the hallway as she walked past the grand staircase and slid back the front door's numerous bolts. Yet, despite her making considerable noise, the knocks became frantic raps.

"*Ooohhh…* please *open* the door!" a low voice cried from the other side.

"I am!" Miss Trent called back, turning the final key. When she opened the door, however, a willowy, gaunt woman stumbled inside with it. Catching her in her arms, Miss Trent felt the contours of the woman's skeleton through her clothes, comprised of a tattered, midnight-blue, woollen shawl over a pale-blue, straight-lined dress. The dress had a high neck and long, narrowed sleeves. Her shawl's edges dripped melted snow onto Miss Trent's blouse, while small puddles formed beneath her heavy, black-booted feet.

"*Ohhhh*," the woman repeated, her voice mimicking her shivering. "Begging your pardon," she added as she straightened and surveyed the damp patch on Miss Trent's blouse. "Miss Trent…?" the woman enquired, meeting Miss Trent's gaze with a look of trepidation in her own. She couldn't have been any older than nineteen, but her mouse-brown hair was streaked with grey. Her thin skin—stretched across angular cheekbones and sunken eye sockets—did her an equal disservice.

"I am she," Miss Trent replied. She closed the door on the falling snow and, sliding a bolt into place, turned toward her visitor. "And you are?"

"Mrs Winnifred Rowe." The woman came

forward, her face contorted with desperation. "I know I'm not expected, Miss Trent, and I can't pay but… I *must* have the Society's help, if I'm to save us from the workhouse."

"As much as I'd like to help, Mrs Rowe, the Bow Street Society's funds aren't as buoyant as they ought to be—"

"But it's *Christmas*!" Mrs Rowe wailed, her voice drawing both Mr Snyder and Miss Dexter from the kitchen.

"Everythin' okay?" Mr Snyder enquired, putting himself between Miss Dexter and the emotional visitor.

"Yes, thank you, Sam," Miss Trent replied. To Mrs Rowe, she explained, "This is Mr Samuel Snyder, a cabman, and Miss Georgina Dexter, an artist. They are both Bow Street Society members." She shifted her gaze back to those she'd introduced, "Mrs Rowe is here to ask for the Society's help. Miss Dexter, could you bring Mrs Rowe and me some tea in the parlour?"

"Of course," Miss Dexter replied with a meek nod.

"Thank you," Miss Trent replied and, indicating the aforementioned room, told Mrs Rowe, "There's a fire you may sit beside."

Mrs Rowe, though dejected, hurried toward the hearth's inviting glow seen through the parlour's open doorway. When she saw the plump, blue sofa set before the fire though, she hesitated.

"Please, sit," Miss Trent invited upon entering behind her.

"I'd rather stand, thank you," came Mrs Rowe's terse—yet nervous—reply.

"Very well," Miss Trent said and took a seat upon an armchair facing the now closed door. Maintaining her calm composure, she continued, "As I'd begun to explain earlier, Mrs Rowe, the Society can't afford to gift monies—even at Christmas. Have you spoken to the parish—?"

"I'm *not* here to *beg*," Mrs Rowe interrupted with

wide eyes. Her grip tightened upon her shawl as she continued, "I want the Society's help. The sort of help it's given others." She darted her eyes around the room and, shifting her weight between her feet, added, "Maybe I oughtn't of come..."

"*Mrs* Rowe," Miss Trent said as she stood.

Mrs Rowe's gaze snapped back to Miss Trent's.

"Please…" Miss Trent began with a smile as she placed her hand upon Mrs Rowe's arm and guided her to the sofa. "Settle down by the fire and tell me what has happened to bring you here."

Mrs Rowe followed Miss Trent to the sofa but wavered as she looked upon its unblemished cushions.

"I wouldn't invite you to sit if I didn't want you to do so," Miss Trent said, her voice gentle, as she witnessed her visitor's trepidation.

"Thank you," Mrs Rowe whispered and sat on the sofa's edge. When the firelight warmed her face, the rigidity fell away from her lips and she bent forward a little. Miss Trent, who had returned to the armchair, watched her entranced visitor in silence. One by one, Mrs Rowe's lean fingers regained their colour while a rosy tinge spread across her cheeks. The dampness of her shawl also waned and, for a time, Mrs Rowe enjoyed some comfort.

"Thank you, Miss Dexter," Miss Trent said as Miss Dexter carried in a tea tray following Mr Snyder's opening of the door.

"You're welcome," Miss Dexter replied with a meek smile while placing the tray on a low table near Miss Trent. Miss Trent again thanked her, and Miss Dexter left with a rustle of her skirts.

"How do you take your tea, Mrs Rowe?" Miss Trent enquired.

"Black… thank you," Winnifred replied.

"Now," Miss Trent began after she'd passed the cup across. "Why have you come to the Bow Street Society today, Mrs Rowe?"

Taking a sip of tea, Winnifred felt its warmth soothe her nerves. All the same, she waited until she'd replaced it upon its saucer before replying, "I work at *Brewer's Toymakers* in the Lowther Arcade—y'know, in the Strand?—well, I *did*, until I was dismissed for—" Her brow furrowed as she glanced toward the ceiling. "…'Improper conduct,' Mr Brewer said." She looked back to Miss Trent and shook her head as she continued, "But I *neva,* in all my years working at the shop, done anything shameful." She straightened, "I'm polite to the customers." She gave a nod. "I smile when I ought." Another nod. "And keep my mouth closed when I ought. I've neva had a bad temper and I don't scowl at the children when they touch the toys."

Her shoulders slumped as she released a loud sigh. "I told Mr Brewer I'd not done what was being said of me, but he paid me no mind. He gave me my pay—on account of it being Christmas—and told me not to go back." She bowed her head, "My Stephen's work don't pay too well, but we always made ends meet. We can't now, though." Putting her cup down, she reached for Miss Trent's arm and looked her square in the eyes. "*Please,* Miss Trent. It's a lot to ask a person but I ask it anyway, not for me but for my children. The work at Brewer's meant the difference between our home and the workhouse."

"I can't guarantee the Society will be able to—"

"*Anything* the Bow Street Society can do for us would be a blessing, Miss Trent. *Anything*!" Mrs Rowe released Miss Trent's arm and added, "My Stephen's a sweep. He'll sweep your chimneys and won't ask for coin."

"That shan't be necessary," Miss Trent replied with a soft smile. "Let me be certain we understand one another, however. You wish for the Bow Street Society to convince Mr Brewer to reemploy you, correct?"

"Yes'm," Mrs Rowe replied.

"The 'improper conduct' you mentioned," Miss Trent said. "What is it you are accused of, exactly?"

"Improper letters to a customer," Mrs Rowe said. Leaning forward, she shook her head and insisted, "But I *neva* done anything of the kind, Miss Trent. I would neva chance losing my work like that—or my Stephen. Lor' *knows* I love him so."

"Very well," Miss Trent said after a few moments' consideration. "The Society accepts your case, Mrs Rowe. Now, take some more tea and warm yourself by the fire until the snow passes. In the meantime, I will send word to some of our Society members who will look into this matter for you."

"*Thank* you, Miss Trent!" Mrs Rowe cried, covering her mouth as tears erupted from her eyes, her body trembled, and her head shook. "*Thank you,* thank you, thank you…"

II

Lowther Arcade, located between West Strand and Adelaide Street, was an impressive structure built—according to *Routledge's Popular Guide to London* (c. 1873)—in the Grecian style. Its interior comprised of a wide corridor lined with several, narrow arches interrupted by higher, clear glass domes. Embossed carvings of flora decorated the corners of each ceiling which curved to meet the domes' edges. The cubed pillars of the arches were embedded into the walls on each side, thus leaving but a few inches to jut outward. The spaces between pillars were occupied by the arcade's many shops, each with identical large, flat-paned, display windows. These windows, constructed from nine individual panes and framed by two Grecian-style pillars, ended at the windows' tops. The doorways into the shops were on one side of these windows. Curled supports for glass sconces—which were similar in shape to a daffodil's trumpet—were mounted upon every other supporting pillar lining the Arcade. At the Arcade's end were three, squared archways formed by two immense, Grecian-style pillars supporting a wall containing three, tall windows. London's streets were beyond these open archways.

In total, the Lowther Arcade was two hundred and forty-five feet long and, in December of 1896, was decorated with boughs and wreaths of holly, laurel, and ivy throughout. The Arcade's toymakers had laid out their wares on stalls outside their respective shop windows. China dolls with painted cheeks, soft dolls stuffed with rags, boxes of wooden toy soldiers, and marionettes were all on display. Majestic fir trees adorned with lit candles and carved angels lined the corridor, filling the cold air with their musky scent.

"God rest ye merry, gentlemen, let nothing you dismay," a choir of well-dressed ladies and top-hatted gentlemen sung as Lady Katheryne Owston and Miss Agnes Webster passed on their way into the Arcade. The shortest singer held a box for donations. With each penny or shilling deposited, she bowed her head and uttered "God bless you." Such was her response when Lady Owston added five pounds to the collection.

In her late forties, Lady Owston's fair complexion remained unblemished by sun or hardship. Though only five feet in height, the black court (or 'Louis') shoes she wore, made her seem taller. Her warm, chestnut-brown hair was styled in tight curls which were, in turn, pinned against her head. A broad-brimmed, pale-yellow, straw hat sat squarely atop her head. Its flourish of white feathers, fresh holly leaves and berries, broad, burgundy ribbon, and green netting increased her height further. Wrapped around her slender—yet wide-shouldered—form was a dark-brown, real fur coat. After depositing her donation, she slipped her black leather-clad hands back into her fur muff and entered the Arcade.

Miss Webster, who'd gifted a few shillings, closed her umbrella and hooked its curved, wooden handle onto the crook of her arm before following her employer. Twenty years of age, Miss Webster's beauty was often described as 'underwhelming' by many who knew her. Nonetheless, her broad, squared shoulders, perfect posture, and hard scrutiny of her surroundings created an unignorably attractive air of strength. Her chocolate-coloured hair was plain, devoid of curls and wrapped into a bun nestled against the base of her skull. Meanwhile the right, front side of her hair was covered by a narrow hat pinned at an unfashionable angle.

In stark contrast to Lady Owston's, Miss Webster's attire comprised of a knee-length, black, cotton cloak over a loosely fitted, cream blouse. This blouse sported the fashionable "leg of mutton" shape (tight on the lower arms, puffed out on the upper). A dark-brown, narrow, brass-buckled belt accentuated her naturally narrow waist. Finally, she wore minimal bustle skirts which had burgundy panels on their front and dark brown, pleated, layers cascading down their back.

An immense throng of people filled the Arcade's corridor. Little girls tugged at the coats of their mothers and governesses while pointing at a doll. Little boys inspected the train sets. Babies slept soundly in their broad-wheeled carriages. Gentlemen discussed quality and price with the toymakers, and the ladies exchanged news of mutual friends.

"Stay close and guard your purse, Agnes," Lady Owston remarked as they joined the masses. "*Brewers* is along here on the left."

"Yes, Lady Owston," Miss Webster replied, following her employer's hat since it was all she could see over the sea of heads. Every so often, someone would cut across her path—a child excited by the displays, pulling along their governess, or a gentleman preoccupied with his pocket watch—forcing Miss Webster to stop or risk collision. It was at those times she was grateful for her employer's flamboyant taste in headwear. Especially as the freelance journalist was in the habit of marching on ahead without ensuring her secretary kept pace.

Shielding her eyes from the fir tree's candles as she passed, Miss Webster joined Lady Owston at the doorway of *Brewer's Toymakers.* Following the example of his competitors, Mr Brewer had set out a stall laden with brightly coloured trains, dolls, puppets, lanterns, and dollhouses.

Standing beside an oak-panelled counter at the shop's rear, Mr Brewer's grey eyes surveyed his domain. Wiry, dark-grey whiskers with off-white patches framed his aged features. Gold-rimmed, round spectacles perched upon the tip of his hooked nose. Beneath his full-frontal, pristine, white apron was a black frock coat and trousers. A broad, black cravat—bookended by a shirt's starched, white collar—peeked out from the apron's top.

Male assistants tended the stall and counter, while two female employees boxed and gift wrapped the purchased toys. Yet, Lady Owston forewent any interaction with the workforce to approach the owner direct.

"Mr Brewer?" she enquired.

"Yes?" the toymaker enquired in return. His voice was a deep baritone, while his eyes gazed upon Lady Owston with keen interest.

"I'm Lady Katheryne Owston, a freelance journalist for the *Truth* and *Women's Signal* publications. This is my secretary, Miss Agnes Webster. In addition to our usual calling, we are members of the Bow Street Society. A former employee of yours—" Lady Owston looked to Miss Webster.

"Mrs Winnifred Rowe," Miss Webster stated.

"Yes! Mrs Winnifred Rowe," Lady Owston repeated, adding to her secretary, "*Thank* you, Agnes. My memory is not what it was." Beaming at Mr Brewer when she faced him again, she continued, "As I was saying... Mrs Winnifred Rowe came to the Bow Street Society in a *terrible* state. *She* claims you dismissed her for improper conduct but, having now met you, Mr Brewer, I sense you are a kind and generous man—one who *recognises* a misunderstanding when he encounters it."

"There's been no misunderstanding," Mr Brewer stated as his genial expression hardened into a scowl. "Mrs Rowe was caught sending an illicit correspondence to one of my wealthiest and loyal customers."

"How was she caught?" Miss Webster enquired, taking a small notebook and pencil from her satchel.

"The customer complained, of course. After he'd found the letter in a box containing the doll he'd purchased for his daughter," Mr Brewer replied.

"May we see the letter?" Miss Webster requested.

Mr Brewer looked between the two ladies. "It shan't do any good. My mind's been made."

"Then our seeing it shan't cause any harm, either," Lady Owston said.

"I'm not aware of its location," Mr Brewer admitted.

"Please look anyway," Miss Webster said.

The toymaker retained his scowl and, after a moment of stubborn inactivity, went behind the counter and rummaged through its drawers. All the while, his workforce moved around him to take customers' monies and gift wrap their purchases. After several minutes—while Lady Owston and Miss Webster were bumped and nudged from all sides—Mr Brewer returned with a single piece of paper. Passing it to Miss Webster, he said, "This is it."

The paper's thickness at once told Miss Webster it was worth more than Mrs Rowe could afford. Written in black ink was the simple question, 'Why do you shun my affection?' The letter was unsigned.

"Do you have this paper in your shop, Mr Brewer?" Miss Webster enquired.

"No," the toymaker replied.

"It's expensive paper," Miss Webster remarked. "How did you come to have the letter?"

"The customer returned it. With the doll and box the doll was packed in. Is that all?"

"Not quite," Lady Owston smiled. "May we have the name—?"

"*Absolutely* not," Mr Brewer barked. "I've said all I have to say, goodbye." Turning toward the counter with a fiercer scowl than before, he stopped, looked over his shoulder at them, and muttered, "And a Merry Christmas." When neither lady spoke, he added, "Will you not wish me the same?"

"Not yet," Lady Owston replied, causing the toymaker's scowl to return.

"*So* be it," he said and walked away.

"Come, Agnes!" Lady Owston announced and, slipping her hands into her muff, turned upon her heel and strode from the shop. "We must return to Bow Street and speak to Miss Trent about what is to be done—"

"Excuse me!" someone called from behind them. As both Lady Owston and Miss Webster looked back, one of the women who'd been wrapping the toys approached. "Begging your pardons," she added when she'd reached them. "I didn't mean to hear what you said to Mr Brewer but, as I was so close by, I couldn't help but overhear. Again, begging your pardons, but it's only right I tell you what I saw."

"What did you see, Miss…?" Lady Owston enquired.

"Libby," the woman replied, pushing a strand of blond hair behind her large ear. "Winnie putting the doll into the box and wrapping it up, but it's what I *didn't* see that I wanted to tell you about." Miss Libby sighed, "Begging your pardons again, ladies, but there *wasn't* a letter or *anything* in the box."

"Have you told Mr Brewer of this?" Lady Owston enquired.

"I have, but he told me to stop meddling."

"The customer who received the doll, may you give us his name?" Miss Webster enquired.

"I… I don't think I ought to," Miss Libby replied with a glance back at the shop.

"It's the only way we can help Mrs Rowe," Lady Owston urged.

"Mr Brewer though…" Miss Libby said, her voice trailing off. Lady Owston and Miss Webster waited, however, and, after some consideration, Miss Libby admitted, "…Lord Monaghan is his name."

"I know of Lord Monaghan," Lady Owston remarked in a dry tone. "Have you served him during his visits?"

"He don't usually come himself. A servant of his does, and buys the toys. Mr Brewer don't approve of us girls speaking with the gentlemen though, or handling the monies. So, neither Winnie nor me have ever talked to him."

Miss Webster's brow quirked at Miss Libby referring to herself as a 'girl'—she was in her early twenties at least.

"You said 'usually.' Has he come in person recently?" Lady Owston queried.

"A couple of days ago," Miss Libby replied. "He came into the shop, spoke to Mr Brewer and then..."

"…And then…?" Miss Webster pressed.

"He had a sort of… funny turn, came over all white. He asked Mr Brewer if any other women worked for him. 'Only Mrs Rowe,' Mr Brewer told him. Lord Monaghan lost even more colour at that. Mr Brewer asked if he was well but he said he was. Then he went off like a rabbit from a hole."

"Does he often buy toys from Mr Brewer?" Lady Owston enquired.

"Yes… but the doll Winnie boxed was the first in weeks," Miss Libby shook her head and grimaced. "The *monies* he's spent on that daughter of his! A fussy one she must be, too."

"Why do you think that?" Lady Owston queried.

"He *never* keeps a doll longer than a day—not the first one he buys anyway. You can be sure his servant will be back the next morning with the doll all wrapped in brown paper in its box. 'Not the hair colour the young mistress wants,' he'd say, or 'The dress is too plain.'"

"Who would take the return?" Miss Webster enquired.

"Winnie did this last time. Before that, it was Miss Kitty, God rest her soul. She was always first in after Mr Brewer and last to leave."

"Thank you, Miss Libby." Lady Owston said, clasping her hands in her own. "Mrs Rowe and the Bow Street Society are *most* grateful for your help. I wish you a *very* Merry Christmas."

"Thank you. A very Merry Christmas to you, too," Miss Libby replied, her face lifting into a smile.

III

"This is exceedingly inconvenient," Lord Monaghan remarked, and pressed his clenched fist to his lips as he gave a hard cough. "You are fortunate I am a curious sort."

He put his fingertips together and laid his elbows upon the broad arms of his chair. Sitting behind a wide, solid-oak desk, he kept his gaze upon Lady Owston—despite Miss Webster sitting at her side. The prominence of his pale-green eyes, long, dark lashes, and rose-red lips made for a notable schism against his powerful build and husky voice.

"Your time is appreciated, Your Lordship," Lady Owston replied.

"Yes, yes… You wish to speak to me of *Brewers*?" More coughing followed. "While it is regrettable she lost her employ, I can only tell you what I told him. The letter was beneath the doll when I opened the box. I was enraged by it so I returned the doll and lodged a complaint."

"Was that the reason for your recent visit?" Lady Owston enquired.

A pause preceded Lord Monaghan's reply. "I don't quite understand."

"You visited *Brewer's Toyshop* after you had already returned the doll," Miss Webster explained.

"*No*. I don't quite understand how it is any of *your* business," Lord Monaghan retorted.

"We mean no offence, Your Lordship. The Bow Street Society is simply trying to assist Mrs Rowe. She vehemently denies any wrongdoing." Lady Owston said.

"As I expected she would," Lord Monaghan replied, stifling yet another cough.

"Why?" Miss Webster enquired. "It's not an act of criminality. What has she to gain?"

"Blast if I know," Lord Monaghan remarked with a weak smile. Clasping his hands upon the desk as he leaned forward, he added, "What is done is done."

"Who were you looking for?" Miss Webster enquired. When the lord remained silent, however, she explained, "You asked after Mr Brewer's employees. You became pale when you were told those in the shop were the only employees Mr Brewer had—except Mrs Rowe."

"It's time for you to leave," Lord Monaghan replied, his lowered voice vicious in its coarseness. Miss Webster straightened and turned her head to gauge her employer's reaction. Lady Owston had lifted her head to look upon the—now standing—lord. He said, "Please, *don't* force my hand."

"We're leaving," Lady Owston replied and, keeping her gaze fixed to his, stood also. "I hope your daughter wasn't too disappointed when she didn't receive a replacement doll."

"My daughter?" Lord Monaghan said, taken aback.

"Yes, the one you purchased all those dolls for. You returned the last doll, Lord Monaghan—the one Mrs Rowe packed—but you didn't get another." Lady Owston pointed out. While Miss Webster put away her things and joined her employer in standing, Lady Owston continued, "If Miss Kitty had taken receipt of your returned doll, you would have certainly been given a replacement." She paused, "Her passing away was a tragedy…"

The two Bow Streeters watched as the colour drained from Lord Monaghan's features. Nonetheless, neither his expression nor his stance altered. Instead, he was as still as the study in which they stood. Lady Owston's lips parted, her shoulders squared, and her head recoiled at his reaction. For a moment, the two just stared at one another—he with his quivering Adam's apple, and she with her held breath. Miss Webster, who had begun to leave, stopped and looked back at the freelance journalist. "Lady Owston…?"

"Lord Monaghan has requested we leave, Agnes," Lady Owston replied, downcast. She gave a small smile when she faced her though. "Let us leave."

"Yes, Milady," Miss Webster replied and opened the study door. Lady Owston's next remark compelled her to pause in the doorway and look back for a second time, however.

"I'm sorry, Your Lordship. Truly," she said.

Lord Monaghan's head gave a slight bob. Without another word, he turned to the wall and dug his fingers into the firm leather of his chair's back. Miss Webster watched him lift his head toward the Heavens but, before she could comment, Lady Owston had taken her arm and steered her from the room.

IV

Hot tea warmed Mrs Rowe's core as she once again sat before the fire in the Bow Street Society's parlour. Attired in drier clothes than her last visit, she admired the fresh holly wreath lining the mantel shelf.

More wreaths and sprigs of mistletoe hung around the room, while a fir tree dominated its back wall. The flames of almost one hundred slender, white candles illuminated its dark green foliage. Standing within shallow holders made of clay painted gold, these candles were prevented from falling by the clay ball suspended beneath them. This ball acted as a counter balance to the top-heavy weight of a melted, wax candle. The balls were, in turn, painted various shades of red, green, and gold. A string of small, brass bells encircled the tree from top to bottom, their surfaces reflecting the dancing fire and candlelight. On the tree's summit was a carved star painted gold. A collection of smaller candles were placed in holders affixed to the branches below the star, thus illuminating it. The tree's base stood within a large, clay pot weighed down with sand. The usually exposed, oak floorboards beneath were covered by a blanket of cotton wool and ivy. Other additions to the parlour were a miniature stable scene on the mantel shelf, a string of Christmas cards hung across the chimney breast, and a bowl of walnuts on the low table.

Mrs Rowe was pulled from her pleasant reverie by the sound of approaching footsteps. When she looked to the door as it opened, however, she was startled by the entrance of her former employer. She stood at once, her eyes wide and her heart racing as the cup she held rattled upon its saucer.

"M—Mr B—Brewer," she said. Glancing at the spilt tea within the saucer, she put both down. "I—I wasn't told of you being here," she added, smoothing her dress and tattered shawl with trembling hands.

"Please be seated, Mrs Rowe," Miss Trent said as

she stepped around the toymaker to enter the parlour. "And you, Mr Brewer."

"Mrs Rowe," the toymaker acknowledged—without looking at her—as he walked past and took the offered armchair.

"This is Lady Katheryne Owston and her secretary, Miss Agnes Webster, Mrs Rowe," Miss Trent introduced when the two Bow Streeters entered next. "I believe you've already met them, Mr Brewer."

"I have," Mr Brewer replied.

"Lady Owston and Miss Webster were assigned to your case, Mrs Rowe," Miss Trent explained. Sitting on a dining chair in the space between the armchair and the sofa—the latter being where Mrs Rowe sat—Miss Trent gestured for her associates to begin.

"Mr Brewer," Lady Owston began, walking forward. When she was certain she had the toymaker's full attention, she continued, "Mrs Rowe is *not* guilty of the moral crime laid at her door. I and Miss Webster are *absolutely* certain of it."

"Oh, thank *goodness*!" Mrs Rowe cried, her hand resting upon her chest.

"*How*?" Mr Brewer challenged. "The letter was found in the box of the doll *she* packed."

"It was, but she didn't put it there," Miss Webster said.

"Lord Monaghan did," Lady Owston added.

Mr Brewer's mouth fell open. "I *beg* your pardon…?"

"Another of your employees—Miss Libby—told us she had *seen* Mrs Rowe box and wrap the doll bought by Lord Monaghan," Lady Owston explained. "Miss Libby said there *wasn't* a letter in the box and *we* are inclined to believe her. Lord Monaghan put the letter in the box before he returned the doll to your shop,"

"I *don't* believe it," Mr Brewer said, his tone and expression hard. "*Why* would he do such a *scandalous* thing?" Mr Brewer turned sharp eyes to Mrs Rowe and demanded, "*What* have *you* been *doing* in *my* shop?"

"She hasn't done *anything*," Miss Webster interjected. When Brewer cast his scowl upon her, she went on, "The letter was intended for the late Miss Kitty— the lady who, according to Miss Libby, would receive Lord Monaghan's returned dolls."

Both Mr Brewer and Mrs Rowe stared at the secretary.

"You forbid any of your employees from speaking with the male customers or handling the monies," Lady Owston said. "The exchange of letters was the only way Lord Monaghan would've been able to communicate with Miss Kitty without you knowing. Given his Lordship's reaction to the news of Miss Kitty's death earlier, he had no knowledge of the fact. We can assume, then, his visit to your shop, Mr Brewer—when he had his turn—was Lord Monaghan trying to find Miss Kitty."

"But… why return the doll? He could've given her the letter in the shop," Mrs Rowe said, clutching and twisting her shawl's corners.

"It could've been seen by Mr Brewer," Miss Webster explained. "I think Lord Monaghan would purchase a doll and Miss Kitty would place a letter in the box with it when she boxed and wrapped it. Then, when Lord Monaghan had written a reply, he would put it under the doll and return the toy with a request for a replacement. When she boxed and wrapped the replacement doll, Miss Kitty must've put her final reply with it."

"Lord Monaghan doesn't have a daughter," Lady Owston announced. "That much was made clear by his confusion when I asked after her."

"What of his not buying anything for weeks?" Mr Brewer enquired, looking between the two Bow Streeters.

"He had rather a bad cough when we saw him," Lady Owston remarked.

"He must've taken ill," Miss Webster interjected.

"And he has admitted to all this?" Mr Brewer enquired.

Lady Owston at once chuckled and, with a slight wave of her hand, replied, "Heavens, *no*! Such a scandal could *ruin* such a man's reputation and the Bow Street Society is *not* in the habit of ruining anyone's name, isn't that right, Miss Trent?"

"It is," Miss Trent replied.

"Lord Monaghan is a lovelorn gentleman who is now nursing a broken heart," Lady Owston resumed. "Besides, our concern was Mrs Rowe and her predicament—a predicament that is now in your power to remedy, Mr Brewer."

"I?" the toymaker replied and, looking about the room, realised all were looking at him. With a frown, he cleared his throat and began, "I'm not entirely certain I can do—"

"*Mr* Brewer," Lady Owston interrupted, raising her voice to drown out Brewer's. Blinking, the toymaker looked up at her. She resumed, "*Need* I remind you of the season? Mrs Rowe is *innocent*. Christmas is not about toys or decorations, but good will to *all* men—*and* women. Would you see a hardworking, *innocent* woman—and her family—in the workhouse at such a time?"

Mr Brewer shifted his gaze to the gaunt, tired face of his former employee.

"*Please*, Mr Brewer. I'll work hard and hold my tongue," Mrs Rowe said.

"No," Mr Brewer replied.

Mrs Rowe's grip upon her shawl tightened.

A ghost of a smile soon passed over the toymaker's lips as he exorcised the scowl. Placing his hand upon the sofa's arm, he smiled. "You will be welcomed back to *Brewer's Toymakers* with open arms. On Christmas Day, you and your family shall dine with me and mine. It's the very *least* I can do."

"*Oh*, Mr *Brewer*!" Mrs Rowe cried, clapping her hand over her mouth to stifle a happy sob. Nevertheless, tears rolled from her eyes and her sobbing strengthened. "*Thank* you," she whispered. Swallowing back her emotion, she looked about the room before standing and going to each person in turn. "*Lady* Owston... Miss *Webster*..." She sniffled, holding one of each lady's hands in her own. Giving them a small squeeze, she whispered, "God *bless* you." Releasing their hands, she turned to clasp Miss Trent's. "...And you, Miss Trent—*thank* you! For *all* you have done." She pulled away and, turning toward them all, added, "It *truly* is a Christmas miracle! God *bless* you *all*!"

Enjoyed the book? Please show your support by writing a review.

**DISCOVER MORE AT...
www.bowstreetsociety.com**

Notes from the author

Spoiler alert

Between work and social commitments, most of us are living increasingly busy lives. As much as we may enjoy snuggling up with a good book, life doesn't always permit us to indulge. Few book lovers are willing to relinquish their addiction entirely, however. Instead, they manage a few pages on the long (or short) train commute to work. It was the book lovers with limited time I had in mind when creating the *Bow Street Society Casebook*. Unlike the main Bow Street Society series of books, these short stories may be fully enjoyed during the small reading window provided by the daily commute.

Consideration for my readers' time restrictions wasn't my only motivation for creating the casebook sub-series though. Whenever I ponder ideas for the main book series, I often come up with concepts for smaller puzzles. While it's true these concepts could be worked into the thread of a wider mystery, more often than not, their impact is in their simplicity. For example, a man who believes he's shrinking at an alarming rate would be— naturally—considered unimportant when one's priority is exposing a brutal murderer. When placed centre stage, in a story of its own, though, this same man's plight becomes far more serious.

In all the casebook short stories, no murders are *actually* committed. Despite Claude being accused of causing Sir Russell's death, he is cleared of all wrongdoing in the end. The other mysteries focus on— arguably—more mundane problems—the unfair dismissal of an employee, the flight of a scared wife from her brutal husband, and the chance encounter with a stranger. What lifts these problems beyond their otherwise mundane status are the circumstances which form them. The employee is dismissed because a letter was found in the box of a doll returned by a wealthy customer, the wife's flight was executed using a devious—yet ingenious—method, and the chance encounter with the stranger was made, seemingly, impossible by the fact the stranger was allegedly dead at the time. All the problems are unusual—uncanny even, in some instances. This, along with the lack of a murder in each short story, was entirely intentional. I wanted to follow in the tradition, first began by Sir Arthur Conan Doyle in his Sherlock Holmes stories, of the quirky problem.

In addition to this, I also wanted to showcase each Bow Street Society members' stock of unique knowledge, and how they use it to investigate and solve crimes. Anyone can ask questions and, if enough are asked, one can guess at the solution. Yet the members featured in these short stories—indeed, the Bow Street Society itself—go one step beyond merely asking questions. They bring their professional experience, life experience, and skills to the task of solving the problem set before them. They utilise each one of these to guide them through the fog of confusion and, ultimately, to the truth. For example, Mr Maxwell recognises Jerome Snelling's nervous disposition due to his own. Additionally, Miss Webster, being Lady Owston's secretary, identifies the monetary value of the paper used to write the damning note found in the doll's box. Even Mr Locke, an illusionist by profession, is able to fathom the 'trick' to Mr Foggity's shrinking. In short, my ultimate goal with these casebook short stories was to demonstrate how *any* skill and/or *any* profession may be turned to detective work.

In so doing, my hope is to demonstrate to *you*, the reader, how the mundane occupation you fulfil day in, day out could have more potential than at first glance. The Bow Street Society's unofficial mantra is: justice by all, for all. One may think one's delivery job is unimportant in life's wider picture. Yet, that same delivery job provides knowledge of streets, shortcuts, and landmarks others may not be aware of—an invaluable skill indeed when following a suspect, or chasing a fleeing villain.

Those living and/or working in London may have recognised many of the locations visited in these stories. Aside from their giving each tale more texture and depth, they also provide another example of how *you*, the reader, may connect with the setting and characters. Rather than being an abstract, fictional entity you may only imagine in your mind's eye, these locations are places you may visit and see for yourself. You may stand upon Bow Street and admire the—now defunct—police station and law court. Oxford Street is one of the world's most famous shopping thoroughfares. St. Katherine's Docks still stand as a monument to London's great shipping past. These physical locations, coupled with the historically accurate descriptions of what they were like in 1896 featured in the casebook stories, further help to bring the Bow Street Society, its members, the cases they investigate, and the era they inhabit to life.

From the very start of my creative journey, through the books and short stories I've written about the Bow Street Society, my aspiration has always been the same. To create a living, breathing universe we may all become close to and lose ourselves in. To transport the reader back to the Victorian era—to help the reader *experience* the streets and people of 1896 London. We're both fortunate and unfortunate in London when it comes to Victorian buildings and locations which still exist in modern times. Unfortunate because many were demolished after World War II, due to bomb damage or slum clearance. Fortunate because many—such as Baker Street station and the Lowther Arcades—still exist, albeit in near unrecognisable incarnations. Nonetheless, we may walk the bridges, wander Oxford Street, and admire the Grecian-style architecture of the Lowther Arcade as Londoners of 1896 would have done.

Put simply, Bow Street Society's London is *our* London. So get out there and do some sightseeing!

~ T.G. Campbell

MORE BOW STREET SOCIETY

The Case of The Peculiar Portrait
& Other Stories
(Bow Street Society Casebook Volume 2)

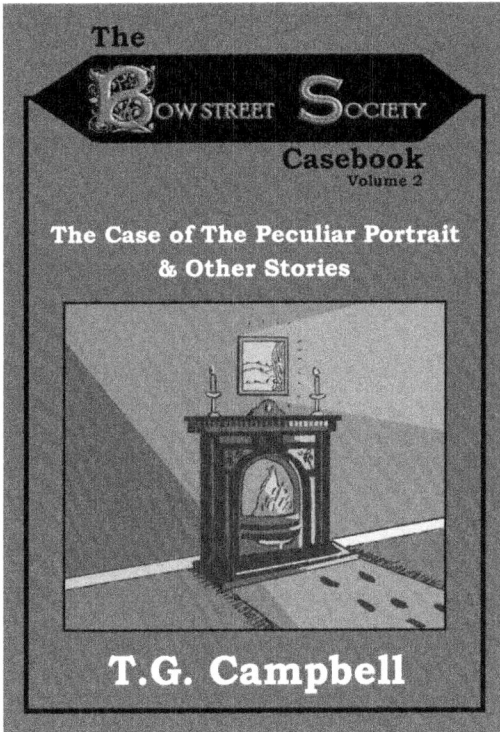

In this second volume, the Bow Street Society investigates more baffling problems posed by a colourful array of clients. Can a crime be solved before it's committed? How have people fallen from a window that can't be opened? How has a dead man disappeared from his own portrait? These are just some of the questions the Bow Street Society must answer to expose the fantastic truths behind these bizarre cases.

In this collection:

The Case of the Desperate Deed
The Case of the Scandalous Somnambulist
The Case of the Chilling Chamber
The Case of the Ghastly Gallop
The Case of the Peculiar Portrait

On sale now in eBook and paperback from Amazon.
Also available for free download via Kindle Unlimited.

The Case of The Russian Rose
& Other Stories
(Bow Street Society Casebook Volume 3)

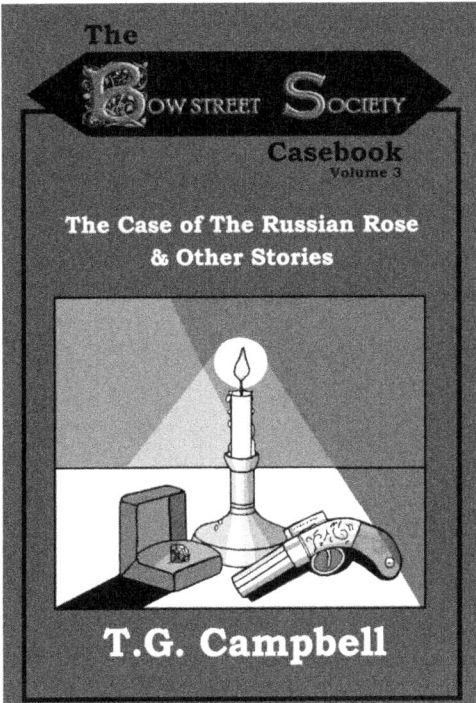

The Case of the Russian Rose & Other Stories is the third volume of shorter mysteries to feature the group. Wherein they must solve peculiar problems posed by their colourful array of clients, such as: "how is a pocket picked in an empty train compartment?" and "How did a bullet vanish from a gun without being fired?" These are just some of the questions the Bow Street Society must answer to expose the fantastic truths behind these bizarre cases

In this collection:

The Case of the Pesky Passenger
The Case of the Taken Teacup
The Case of the Russian Rose
The Case of the Crooked Cottage
The Case of the Baffled Bride

On sale now in eBook and paperback from Amazon.
Also available for free download via Kindle Unlimited.

The Case of The Gentleman's Gambit
& Other Stories
(Bow Street Society Casebook Volume 4)

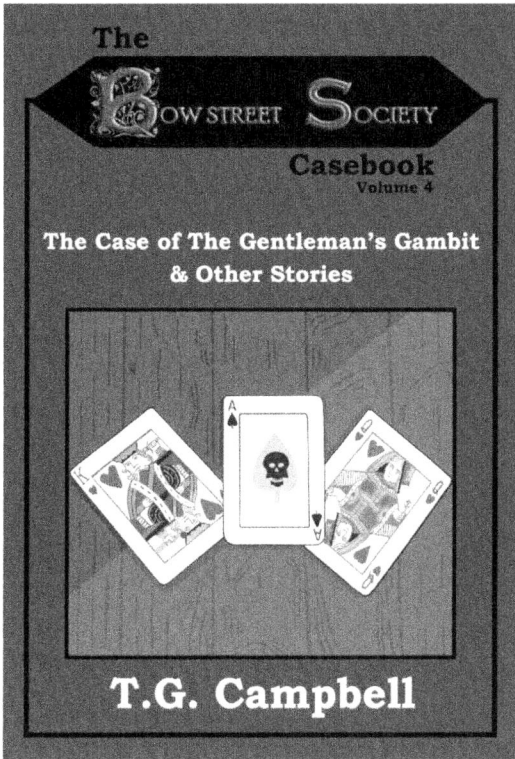

The Case of the Gentleman's Gambit & Other Stories is
the fourth volume of shorter mysteries to feature the
group. Wherein they must solve peculiar problems posed
by their colourful array of clients, such as: "how did gold
vanish from a moving train without four guards seeing the
thief?", "Is a ghost from Whitechapel haunting a wealthy
woman?" and "Can playing cards be used to poison
someone?" These are just some of the questions the Bow
Street Society must answer to expose the fantastic truths
behind these bizarre cases.

In this collection:

The Case of the Terrific Theft
The Case of the Whitechapel Wraith
The Case of the Fowler Fortune
The Case of the Gentleman's Gambit
The Case of the Puma Problem

On sale now in eBook and paperback from Amazon.
Also available for free download via Kindle Unlimited.

SOURCES OF REFERENCE

A great deal of time was spent researching the historical setting of the short stories in the *Bow Street Society Casebook*. This research covered not only the physical setting of London in 1896, but also communication technology (such as typewriters and telephones), medicine, the Metropolitan Police, and architects, to name but a few. Thus, a great deal of information about the period has been gathered, to inform me of the historical boundaries of my characters' professions and lives, which hasn't been directly referenced in this book. Where a fact, or source, has been used to inform the basis of in-book descriptions of interiors, and street items, *et cetera,* I've strived to cite said source here. Each citation includes the source's origin, the source's author, and the part of a short story the source is connected to. The citations are, in turn, grouped under the name of the *Bow Street Society Casebook* short story they are connected to. All rights connected to the following sources remain with their respective authors and/or publishers.

The Case of the Shrinking Shopkeeper

Baren, Maurice <u>Victorian Shopping</u> (Michael O'Mara Books Limited, London, 1998) "From Small Acorns…" Chapter, pp.20-30
Mrs Foggity's reference to successful confectioners in the north. Lemonade in the Foggity's Sweet Shop.

<u>"Victorian Sweets"</u> information sheet downloaded from:
www.shcg.org.uk/domains/shcg.org.uk/local/media/.../victorian_sweets___notes.doc
"These notes are taken from a training pack written for staff at York Castle Museum working in the re-created Terry's sweetshop." – Text on document.

Description of confectionary types for sale in Mr Foggity's shop.

The Case of the Winchester Wife

Reynolds' Shilling Coloured Map of London, 1895, a copyright-free, contemporary reference source from Lee Jackson's Victorian Dictionary website:
http://www.victorianlondon.org/index-2012.htm
The Great Northern Company and King's Cross being a terminus.

Cruchley's London in 1865: A Handbook for Strangers, 1865, a copyright-free, contemporary reference source from Lee Jackson's Victorian Dictionary website:
http://www.victorianlondon.org/index-2012.htm
Trains from King's Cross travelling to York.

The Case of the Perilous Pet

Encyclopædia Britannica's article, *Neoclassical architecture*, by The Editors of Encyclopædia Britannica.
https://www.britannica.com/art/Neoclassical-architecture
Mr Heath's classification of Russell Hall as being an example of Neoclassicism and Mr Heath's remarks about the popularity of this style of architecture.

Conformation diagram for Staffordshire Bull Terrier
Dr Alexander's examination of Claude, specifically the various parts of his body.

Popular Stairs.com's article, *Stairs Types*.
http://popularstairs.com/basic-stair-building/stairs-types
The name of the stair type Sir Russell fell down, Mr Heath's explanation of it, and Mr Heath's remark regarding the number of steps in a flight of stairs.

The Case of the Eerie Encounter

Historic England's article, *Baker Street station: main entrance building and metropolitan, circle and Hammersmith and city line platforms (no's 1-6) including retaining wall to approach road.*
https://historicengland.org.uk/listing/the-list/list-entry/1239815
History of Baker Street station's construction.

Leisure Hour: UNDER LONDON TOWN, 1862, a copyright-free, contemporary reference source from Lee Jackson's Victorian Dictionary website:
http://www.victorianlondon.org/index-2012.htm
Skylights and eyelet holes.

Cassells Household Guide, New and Revised Edition (4 Vol.) c.1880s [no date] - Domestic Medicine…(9) Apoplexy. Asthma, a copyright-free, contemporary reference source from Lee Jackson's Victorian Dictionary website:
http://www.victorianlondon.org/index-2012.htm
Treatment of asthma in the Victorian era, specifically drinking a cup of strong coffee, inhaling the smoke of burning brown paper soaked in salt-petre (nitrate of potash), and having a change of air.

Thoughtco.com's article, *Saltpeter or Potassium Nitrate*
https://www.thoughtco.com/saltpeter-or-potassium-nitrate-608490
Most common modern day term for Saltpeter, the modern use of Saltpeter as a food preservative, and fact the chemical is toxic in high doses.

The Case of the Christmas Crisis

Summary of the observations made at the stations included in the daily and weekly weather reports, for

the calendar month, December 1896. (Issued as a Supplement to the Weekly Weather Report, 1896.) from the UK Met Office website.
https://www.metoffice.gov.uk/binaries/content/assets/mohippo/pdf/9/2/dec1896.pdf
"Earthquake shock" on 17th December across England and Wales, specifically in the western counties.

Cassells Household Guide, New and Revised Edition (4 Vol.) c.1880s [no date] - Christmas Decorations of the Home a copyright-free, contemporary reference source from Lee Jackson's Victorian Dictionary website:
http://www.victorianlondon.org/index-2012.htm
The Christmas decorations Miss Dexter and Miss Trent are making using brown paper, twine, holly, laurel, and ivy.

Grace's Guide to British Industrial History: 1896 London-Brighton Run
https://www.gracesguide.co.uk/1896_London-Brighton_Run
Though it isn't mentioned by Mr Snyder in the story, the first London to Brighton Run was organised by the Motor Car Club and held on the 14th November 1896. This is the event Mr Snyder is referring to.

Routledge's Popular Guide to London: BAZAARS AND ARCADES, (c.1873) a copyright-free, contemporary reference source from Lee Jackson's Victorian Dictionary website:
http://www.victorianlondon.org/index-2012.htm
Description of the Lowther Arcade being built in the Grecian style.

Lowther Arcade: Interior view (1832) wood engraving. City of London Collage (London Met. Archives). Catalogue No: SC_PZ_WE_01_1559

https://collage.cityoflondon.gov.uk/view-item?key=SHsiUCI6eyJzdWJqqZWN0X2lkIjoxMjMzMyw iam9pbl9vcCI6Mn19&pg=8&WINID=1510247073789#C s3bp3SqdgwAAAFfob2PaQ/309048
Lowther arcade's interior description.

London Met. Archives Collage. Lowther Arcade: Christmas shoppers purchasing toys (1870) wood engraving. Catalogue No: SC_PZ_WE_02_0678
https://collage.cityoflondon.gov.uk/view-item?i=312751&WINID=1510247073789
Description of Christmas trees in Lowther Arcade.

Black's Guide to London and Its Environs, (8th ed.) 1882. a copyright-free, contemporary reference source from Lee Jackson's Victorian Dictionary website:
http://www.victorianlondon.org/index-2012.htm
Length of Lowther Arcade.

Christmas Tree Candleholders, Victoriana Magazine
http://www.victoriana.com/christmas/christmascandlehold ers.htm
Description of candles and suspended balls beneath on Christmas tree in the Society's parlour.

Printed in Great Britain
by Amazon

59457195R00067